DINOTOPIA®
SURVIVE!

by Brad Strickland

Random House 🏠 New York

For Ray Bradbury,
who loves dinosaurs.

RANDOM HOUSE and colophon are registered trademarks of Random House, Inc.

www.randomhouse.com/kids
www.dinotopia.com

Library of Congress Cataloging-in-Publication Data
Strickland, Brad.
Survive! / by Brad Strickland.
   p. cm. — (Dinotopia)
SUMMARY: Twelve-year-old Kurt and his father encounter poisonous plants,
an earthquake, and a gigantic flesh-eating dinosaur when they begin exploring
the interior of the Outer Island near Dinotopia.
ISBN 0-375-81108-7   [1. Dinosaurs—Fiction.   2. Islands—Fiction.
3. Adventure and adventurers—Fiction.   4. Fantasy.]   I. Title.   II. Series.
PZ7.S9166 Su 2001   [Fic]—dc21   00-62550

RL: 6.2

Printed in the United States of America   April 2001   10 9 8 7 6 5 4 3 2 1

DINOTOPIA IS A REGISTERED TRADEMARK OF JAMES GURNEY

Cover illustration by Michael Welply

DINOTOPIA®

SURVIVE!

Windy Point

Crystal Caverns •

The Hatchery •

Baz •

Pooktook •

Volcaneum •

Hadro
Swamp

Waterfall City •

Sculpted Cliffs •

Cornucopia •   *Deep Lake*
Treetown •   • Bent Root

Solongo River

Temple Ruins •.

RAINY
BASIN
GREAT CANAL

NORTHERN PLAINS

BACKBONE MOUNTAINS

Rocky Pass   Prosperine •   *Sapphire Bay*

• Poseidos
(sunken)

CRACKSHELL POINT

Amra River

SKY GALLEY CAVES •

Tentpole of the Sky •

Sky City •
Thermala •

• The Time Towers

★ Sauropolis

Dolphin Bay

Canyon City •

Ancient Gorge

Red Rapid
Canyon

The Portal

Pteros

The Sentinels

GREAT DESERT

Warmwater
Bay

Culebra •

OUTER ISLAND

FORBIDDEN MOUNTAINS

Dragonfly Coast

BLACKWOOD
FLATS

• Chandara

Cape Turtletail

CHAPTER 1

Kurt Ramos gripped the wicker rail and stared down at the rapidly shrinking figures on the ground. Half a dozen humans and eight dinosaurs craned back to watch the compact sky galley soar. The humans waved, though some shook their heads in doubt. No one ever took a sky galley to the interior of Outer Island. At least no one ever had before.

"Kurt!" his father, Stanhope Ramos, called sharply. "Tostri and I could use your leg power."

"Sorry, Father." Kurt swung around and into the saddle. Backward. He put his feet on the pedals and began to crank them. Facing him was his Deinonychus friend Tostri. His father sat in the front of the gondola, just behind the backward-facing Kurt. With a grin, Kurt said to Tostri, "Let's see how fast we can make this thing fly!"

Tostri's nostrils flickered in amusement. His clawed hands moved in a rapid pattern of gestures and signs: *This is not a race, my friend. Endurance will get us to Rugged Ridge, not speed. Besides, I like this pace. It's been a long time since I ran easily for miles, and that is just what my legs were built for! Pedaling is the next best thing.*

Kurt raised his voice and called out to his father: "Tostri's enjoying the ride, but I'd like to go a little faster. Could we?"

People who did not know the Ramos family might have marked Stanhope Ramos as a man who spent all his time outdoors. Muscular and bearded, he looked like a miner or a woodsman. Those who had met him, however, quickly learned that the tall, dark man with curly black hair was really a healer, and a gentle one at that. To Kurt, though, he could be a strict father. Now he grunted impatiently. "No need to tire ourselves. The breeze will take us in the right direction and should get us there well before sunset. We just have to keep enough thrust to steer."

Tostri signed again: *The answer is no?*

Kurt sighed and nodded.

The Deinonychus made one last comment: *Then you had better turn around. Use your breath to pedal properly, not to talk, and we will get there all the faster!*

Before he did, Kurt took a long look around and behind. Overhead, the helium-filled bag made crinkling noises as the gas inside expanded with altitude, and the ropes creaked. The two propellers on either side of the crew gondola whispered as they spun. Up here at three hundred feet, the land noises had all but vanished.

Already, Culebra, the only major settlement on Outer Island, had drifted away behind. Probably, Kurt thought, the dinosaurs and humans who had seen them off were already back to their own concerns. Beyond the harbor city of Culebra lay the misty surface of Warmwater Bay, and even beyond that the dim, foggy coast of Dinotopia.

Swinging himself easily around in the saddle, Kurt began to pedal hard. Ahead of them the land rose. His father dumped some ballast, and the sky galley jumped to five hundred feet, then a thousand. No wonder his father had christened the craft *Cloud-climber*!

Pedaling hard, watching his father's back, Kurt wondered if this might be the right time to bring up the question of his future. He dreaded the moment and had postponed it again and again. Even if his father agreed, Kurt thought, it would be with a sense of hurt and betrayal. But would he agree? Stanhope Ramos was a determined man, and he could be a stern one. Still, what he said and did could determine Kurt's whole future.

Now they sailed over a deep green rainforest canopy, the details of which were lost in the distance. Occasionally, the surface threw sounds up with startling clarity: the shriek of an Archaeopteryx, the thunder of a waterfall. The sun was in the west, and the inland breeze was about as strong as it would get. Kurt could see only fair-weather clouds, small puffy balls of cumulus. No towering, anvil-headed storm clouds. They were what his father's friends had most feared when Stanhope Ramos had announced his intention of checking out a rumor about the trees on Rugged Ridge. Everyone knew that a storm could tear a sky galley to ribbons in the blink of an eye. And everyone knew that storms were far from predictable.

Still, Stanhope Ramos had a definite goal in mind, based on tales travelers from Culebra had brought to Waterfall City. If the stories were true, all along the summit of a fifteen-mile-long ridge grew a flourishing forest of rockwillow. That was a variant subspecies of *Salix pentandra,* a willow that grew in widely scattered groves on the mountain slopes of Dinotopia. Unlike its cousin the weeping willow, *Salix pentandra* grew best under dry conditions.

But like the weeping willow, the rockwillow's bark yielded an extremely potent pain and fever reducer. The tree was rare in Dinotopia, but the Outer Island strain might just be tough enough to propagate and grow, if only Stanhope and Kurt could bring back viable specimens. "And besides," Stanhope had rumbled to Kurt's mother and to a gathering of his friends, "who knows what other useful medicines we may discover there? No healer has ever explored the ridge. It's certainly worth the small risk."

Well—*any* risk was worth it, in Kurt's opinion, as long as it broke up the monotony of his apprenticeship. Kurt's father was determined that his only son was going to be a healer. Indeed, at age twelve, Kurt was already capable of stitching up a human or saurian wound. He could set a broken limb and diagnose half a hundred common disorders. These and other medical tasks he dealt with competently.

If only he didn't have to.

Again the words almost formed themselves on Kurt's tongue: "Father, we have to talk about my apprenticeship." And again worry about what the tall man might say choked them off. *Soon,* Kurt promised himself. *I will speak to him soon.*

Kurt shifted on his saddle as the afternoon sun made him squint. This was what he really liked, being outside, exploring, seeing new things. Oh, he supposed he would be a capable enough healer in time, but his heart was not in the prospect. He most enjoyed being on his own, or in the silent company of his best friend, Tostri, who at the age of five years was an adolescent. For his part, Tostri, who had been born without the ability to speak or hear, seemed to relish the company of his human friend. The other deinonychids of his age ignored him, not cruelly, but simply because he could not easily follow their speech. So Tostri had become something of a loner, at least before he met Kurt. And, like Kurt, the young dinosaur loved running, climbing, and probing the secrets of Dinotopia. To be an explorer––

"Lean left!" His father's voice rang sharply, and Kurt gestured with his left arm to pass the word along to Tostri. Then they all leaned as Stanhope Ramos brought the airship around in a slow curve. As they had risen, so had the land below. Now they sailed along only a hundred feet above the treetops. This was Rugged Ridge, and it snaked away to the east and north, toward the great fissured cone of Brightfire Mountain. Kurt could see the peak, dimmed by mist, but crowned with a towering plume of white steam. The ancient volcano still packed enough energy to give occasional displays of brilliant yellow and orange lava fountains, though no serious eruption had occurred in living memory. Kurt noted that the column of steam rose lazily, only a little out of vertical line. That meant the wind was holding well for them.

He didn't doubt they would reach their destination, assuming they spotted the rockwillow forest. That would be the easy part. Harder would be securing the *Cloudclimber* for the thirty-six hours or so they would need. They could tether it to trees, but a strong, unexpected gust might tear its moorings or even rip the gasbag. They carried three cylinders of compressed gas in case the bag developed small leaks, but that was nowhere near enough to let them lift off again. And an overland march back to Culebra would be difficult and dangerous. Unlike Dinotopia, Outer Island was not a place where, when a dinosaur met a human, the automatic greeting would be "Breathe deep, seek peace." No, on this isolated island, the response might be more like a roar and a run for life.

No one really knew. Except for one recent expedition, the interior of the island remained a mystery.

Kurt's imagination worked overtime to fill in the gaps. He saw himself as the hero, saving his dad and Tostri from all kinds of dangers. If the *Cloudclimber* came to grief, or if some other disaster happened, he would lead the party back to civilization, braving all unknown dangers—

"Pay attention, son!"

Kurt started from his daydream. "What?" He turned to see his father gesturing impatiently.

"To the right," he said. "We'll set down there."

Surprised at the ache in his knees, Kurt realized they had been pedaling for hours. The red sun was already only a hand's breadth from the horizon. Brightfire Mountain loomed a few miles ahead and to their right. Now Kurt could see that its ancient flanks were cut by deep gullies and defiles that became steep-sided valleys radiating through the rainforest. Silver glints of river shone from the depths of many. Here Rugged Ridge curved away westward from the distant mountain, ran north, and then in the far, misty distance swerved back to the east again.

The trees below them certainly looked like laurel willows. Their broad, rounded crowns swayed in the afternoon breeze; their long spear-point leaves fluttered, now glossy, dark green, now paler, as the top or the bottom surface showed. Kurt saw the landing place his father had in mind: a clearing at the midpoint of the ridge, a bare rocky surface where no tree could find roothold. Kurt turned in the saddle again and quickly told Tostri they had arrived. The Deinonychus kept both eyes focused on Kurt's lips, reading the words they spoke.

"Tired?" Kurt finished with a grin, knowing his dinosaur friend too much to doubt the reply.

Tostri signed, *I could do this for days. You and your father see to the ladder. I will take care of our speed and position.*

To descend from a sky galley, one had to throw a rope ladder over one side (in this case the starboard side), while counterbalancing the weight of the climber with a bag of ballast, usually sand, lowered from the opposite side. Kurt's father handled the ballast, and by arm signals, he helped Tostri maneuver to the best spot. Then the Deinonychus used his powerful hind legs to reverse the thrust of the propellers and hold the blimp almost stationary, fifty feet above the rocky clearing.

Kurt let himself slide down the rope ladder, disdaining to use the rungs. He hit the ground with a solid but not painful thump and immediately secured a line to the nearest tree trunk. It happened to be a rockwillow, he noted.

More lines spiraled down from the gondola, and before long, Kurt had tethered the *Cloudclimber* to half a dozen trees. Then his father descended the ladder (more slowly, Kurt noticed, than he had come) and helped Kurt rig the pulleys that would give them the leverage to tow the airship down. After half an hour's work, each of them hauled on a line, and the craft settled unwillingly into the clearing. Then Tostri leaped out with a bound and helped run still more lines over the top of the gasbag. In Dinotopia, sky galleys docked in caverns, safe from random winds. Outer Island offered no handy caverns, and so they had to do the best they could.

"An hour of daylight left—maybe two!" exclaimed Kurt's father, dusting his hands and staring at the sky with satisfaction. "Kurt, you and Tostri set up camp. I want the campfire site at the far end of the clearing, downwind. There's plenty of loose stone, so build up a deep fire pit. I don't want any stray sparks blowing out. We're here to find medicines, not to start a forest fire."

Kurt nodded as he and Tostri began to unpack the gondola. Stanhope headed straight for the trees, murmuring, "Remarkable! An entirely different subspecies."

Setting up a tent and building a fire pit were tasks that Tostri and Kurt had done a hundred times. They finished with ample daylight to spare. Kurt hunkered over the fire pit, arranging kindling and deadfall wood in it.

"I wonder where the dangers are?" he asked Tostri. "All I've seen so far are some curious rock pigeons."

Tostri tilted his head. His hands moved rapidly.

Predators do live in places like this. But I sense no sign of them. Still, we must be careful. We know meat-eaters do roam the rainforest here.

"Maybe we can go down there. Sort of a side trip." Kurt glanced at Tostri from the corner of his eyes, wondering mischievously how the Deinonychus would react.

No side trips! his friend signed sternly. *I do not know about you, but I do not wish to end up as a side dish!*

"Come on," Kurt teased. "The worst thing we could run into would be a carnivorous dinosaur. Like yourself."

Not like me! Tostri insisted. *Here they would be like the dinosaurs in the Rainy Basin. Some of them may hunt just for sport!*

Kurt frowned. That was hard for him to understand. Sport was doing something physical that you enjoyed just to show your skills and to improve them. You played sports because it felt good and hurt no one. How could hunting, killing, be a *sport*? It simply didn't sound Dinotopian. But then, he reflected, Tostri really knew no more about Outer Island than he did. It was all too easy for ignorance to breed doubts and fears.

Stanhope Ramos emerged from a stand of willows, clutching a damp cloth. "Slips," he explained as he carefully removed a dozen small strips of willow. He placed these in thin earthenware containers, thrusting them down into moist earth taken from around the roots of the parent trees. "With luck, these will take root. I want to get a hundred more tomorrow. We'll have to test the properties of the bark back home in Waterfall City, but I think our chances are good. These look very much like the rockwillows on the west ridges of the Forbidden Mountains."

Kurt said, "Those make the best fever tea in Dinotopia."

His father nodded in agreement. "But they're so rare that the willows are themselves endangered. This seems a much hardier variant, if only it has the same properties."

Tostri had the fire going, an economical blaze that sent up little smoke and no sparks. He raised his chin in token of asking a question and signed, *Congratulations, Healer Ramos! But if we cannot eat those slips of willow, may we eat some of our supplies? I'm starving!*

So was Kurt. Pedaling the *Cloudclimber* for more than six hours had left him ravenous. They rigged a cooking tripod and soon had a hanging pot of stew simmering over the red-hot coals. It bubbled and hissed and gave off a wonderful aroma. The thick soup contained no meat, but it did contain a mixture of lentils and maize that provided plenty of protein. Along with that were a rich blend of vegetables, including some sun-dried tomatoes, whose remote ancestors had come to Dinotopia aboard an outrigger craft from Middle America.

When Kurt tasted the stew, the satisfying tang reminded him of a toasted bread covered with tomato paste and mastodon cheese the Skybax rider Will Denison had once shared with him. Unlike his father, Kurt occasionally ate seafood, eggs, and cheese or butter. As was the case with many healers, Stanhope Ramos was a complete vegetarian.

Tostri's clan were meat-eaters, but Tostri himself seemed just as happy to share the Ramos family's fare. He ate his share of the stew—a somewhat bigger portion than Kurt's or his father's, because Tostri had done more work. And he was ready for seconds, nodding his head and flicking his tongue to show how tasty he thought the simple meal was. When they had finished, dark was closing in.

As he put more wood on their small campfire, Kurt took a deep breath. Then he said, "Father, Tostri has been talking to his parents about training with the Explorers—"

"Good," Stanhope said. "As much as we know about Dinotopia, there is still much to learn. The Explorers do valuable work, even as we healers do."

"I like exploring, too," Kurt said.

"As a healer, you will have chances to explore," Stanhope said. "Expeditions like this one."

Kurt gave Tostri a look of despair. His father wouldn't even listen to him. With a sigh, he said, "Yes, Father."

Tostri shook his head sympathetically. Then he stretched and asked, *Who shall keep the first watch? I will be pleased to do so if you wish.*

"Then wake me in four hours," Kurt's father said with a chuckle. "And thank you for volunteering!"

Kurt sighed. That meant he would get the third watch. He would be the one awake to see the dawn. Well, that meant he needed to sleep while he could. He and his father had dragged piles of dry willow leaves from under the trees. Now they spread their sleeping mats over the leaves and turned in. The night wind blew fitfully up on the ridge, and Kurt could hear the creaks and strains of the *Cloudclimber's* tether lines. They seemed to be holding, though. He fell asleep with no fears for the sky galley.

A few seconds later, or so it seemed to Kurt, his father shook him awake. "Your turn," he said softly.

"Already?" mumbled Kurt. But he rose stiffly, anyway. The willow leaves had been fragrant, but not very soft. Not with solid rock beneath them! Kurt stretched and shivered. The predawn air was cool.

"Keep a low fire going," his father said. "Neither Tostri nor I saw any sign of danger, but stay alert, anyway."

Kurt wrapped a blanket around his shoulders. "I will." He yawned, turned around, and froze. "Father!"

Stanhope Ramos sat straight up. "What?"

Raising an arm, Kurt pointed. "Fire!"

13

His father chuckled. "Correction. Brightfire. Brightfire Mountain, to be precise. It's a lava display, that's all. Good night."

Kurt heard his father settle back down. He walked to the edge of the clearing and stared into the distance. Miles away, jets and fountains of what looked like liquid fire leaped and capered. Their light was bright enough to show him occasional flickering glimpses of the rainforest canopy in the valleys radiating from the volcano. The sight was eerie and somehow disturbing. Turning from the display, Kurt carefully stacked a little more wood on their own fire. Then he walked back to the *Cloudclimber* and made sure that her moorings were secure. Everything felt taut.

Then, with his back to the volcano, Kurt saw the gasbag above him light up clearly in a bright orange glare. He spun and realized that an enormous fountain of lava had just burst from the volcano. It was far larger and brighter than any he had yet seen. It must have jetted hundreds of feet into the air.

The brilliance of the white-hot liquid rock faded as the fountain broke apart and fell back to the volcano's flanks. Seconds passed. Then a low rumble rose and became a distant roar, like breakers on a rocky shore.

And then Kurt staggered as the rock beneath his feet shivered and vibrated.

"It's nothing," he told himself as the lurching subsided. "Just a shock from the volcano. Nothing to worry about."

As minutes drew out, he decided he was right. Though Brightfire Mountain still smoldered and glowed, it sent out no more huge jets of lava, caused no more earth tremors. Nothing to worry about.

But settling the question *did* keep him awake until dawn and the end of his watch.

CHAPTER 2

"Father," Kurt asked after breakfast, "do you need our help?"

Stanhope Ramos smiled at his son. "I know what you're really asking," he said in his rumbling voice. "You want to know if you and Tostri can go exploring! Wouldn't you rather help me here? I can tell you about the process of making fever tea. You'll need that knowledge as a healer."

Kurt took a deep breath. Had the right time come at last? He couldn't meet Stanhope's gaze as he said softly, "Father, I don't know if I'll ever become a healer like you."

His father patted his shoulder. "You'll gain the skills in time. You will get better and better as you study. I wasn't certain I could learn all a healer must know, either, but patience paid off. After all, you have a long heritage as a healer. You will make your family proud."

Feeling like a traitor to all his ancestors, Kurt said, "I know that you are proud of what you do. Everyone honors you for your abilities. But I—well, I'm not sure I *want* to be a healer."

There. He had said it. Kurt waited for his father to reply. At last he looked up.

Stanhope Ramos was gazing at him with a surprised expression. "No?" he asked softly. "Our family has always produced healers, son. What else would you be?"

Kurt shook his head. He wanted to tell his father that he was only twelve, that what he wanted to be changed from year to year. Right now he thought he would be happy as an explorer, but would that be true next year? He could remember wanting to be a Skybax rider not so long ago. He confessed, "I'm not sure. But today—today, sir, I'd rather go exploring with Tostri."

His father turned away from him. In a gruff voice, he said, "Well, you may go. I can gather more slips from the rockwillows easily enough, and who knows? You may discover something interesting. Keep an eye out for any unfamiliar plants. But be sure you're always within calling distance. And stay on the ridge! No climbing down the cliff face, even if you see a tempting specimen."

"All right," Kurt agreed. *He's upset,* Kurt could not help thinking. *He sounds almost angry.* "We won't take any chances, I promise. Thanks, Father." He slung a leather collection pouch over his shoulder. Turning to his friend, he tried to put a convincing smile on his face as he said, "Tostri, Father says we can explore."

First, Tostri replied, *let us make certain our fire is out.*

It didn't take long to douse their campfire with water and to cover its damp ashes with a layer of dry soil. By then, Stanhope Ramos was deep in a thicket of rockwillow, happily gathering shoots.

Kurt looked around and then gestured toward the north, where the ridge climbed toward a rocky overhang. It was like a stony balcony overlooking the rainforest below. Tall conifers grew there, their green crowns brilliant in the morning light. "This way," Kurt said. He and Tostri began to climb.

The slope was not great, though to their right, the cliff dropping down to the rainforest grew steeper and more forbidding. Soon they had left the stand of rockwillows behind and entered a stretch growing thick with thorny creepers and small pines. Kurt's greatest difficulty was breaking through the occasional clump of head-tall saplings. At one point, their path took them over a slippery expanse of dark gray volcanic stone—probably a bad place in a thunderstorm, Kurt thought. All around him were bowl-shaped depressions where lightning bolts had blasted into the rock in ages past. Still the two friends worked their way upward. Soon Kurt was breathing hard, but the exertion felt good.

Just short of their goal, Kurt paused and looked back. The white fabric sausage of the *Cloudclimber*'s gasbag stood out sharply against the trees to which they had tethered the sky galley. Stanhope Ramos was close by, kneeling as he packed away his collection of slips. He glanced up, seemed to notice Kurt, and waved.

Kurt returned his wave and then felt Tostri nudge him. He turned to his friend. "Yes?"

Are you tired? Tostri asked. *I know you humans don't have much endurance.*

Kurt shook his head, though the climb had broken him into a sweat. "I was just checking to make sure we hadn't strayed too far from camp. I'm not tired at all," he said. "Want to race?"

Not here! Tostri signed emphatically. They continued upward, following the crest of the ridge. Underfoot, bare stone gave way to thin, gritty soil. From it grew ferns, and then, as they reached their goal, stands of trees.

When they stood on the overhang itself, Tostri tilted his head meaningfully in the direction of the rainforest, its treetops now six hundred feet below them. *We must be careful here.*

Kurt shaded his eyes. The ridge fell away both to his right and to his left. No rockwillows grew here, but there were many conifers, most of them tall with shaggy bark. A few were squat and more firlike. At their roots, where the soil must have been thickest, clumps of smaller plants waved in the breeze. Kurt turned toward Tostri. "Let's look around. I want to check out the mosses and low plants under those trees. We might find something new."

So for a little while, they searched. They turned up nothing especially interesting. The lichens, fungi, and ferns were the same as in the mountainous areas of Dinotopia. But then, under the shade of the trees, something brittle crunched under Kurt's foot. It felt like an eggshell. Curious, Kurt used his toe to scrape away a layer of dusty reddish brown pine needles, revealing what lay beneath.

Bones. He had stepped onto the skeleton of a small bird, crushing the tiny skull. And now that he was looking for bones, Kurt saw them all over. Most were bird bones, delicate and dry. A few looked like the bones of small mammals, mice or shrews. Some were very recent, some many months old, splotched green and gray, and crumbling with rot and mold. "I wonder what killed these creatures?" Kurt asked. He realized he didn't have Tostri's attention and moved to face his friend. "Look at the bones," he said, pointing down. "What do you suppose killed them?"

Tostri leaned close and sniffed at some of the bleached gray-white skeletons. Then he straightened, his keen eyes puzzled. He signed, *I cannot tell. Some small predator? Yet the bones have not been chewed.*

Kurt felt a prickling along his spine. He looked away, toward the distant cone of Brightfire Mountain. He turned back to Tostri. "Maybe—maybe the volcano?" he hazarded. "Poisonous gases?"

Tostri stared at the smoldering volcano. Then he made a gesture of doubt. *I do not think so. Surely not this far from the source. And no one we met in Culebra told any stories of poisons from Brightfire Mountain, and they told us of every danger they could name! This is a puzzle.*

They cast about under the tall conifers and found even more bones, some of them fresher, some so old that they had weathered almost to dust. The most recent bird skeleton still had blotched gray traces of skin and a few long white primary feathers clinging to it. The bird had been a gull, perhaps pausing here as it migrated across Outer Island.

"I'll tell Father about this," Kurt decided. He looked around and realized that Tostri's attention was elsewhere. The Deinonychus was standing a few feet away. He was on tiptoe, one hand resting on the trunk of a pine. He stared upward.

Kurt joined Tostri and touched his arm. "What is it?" he asked his dinosaur friend.

Tostri rapidly signed, *About halfway to the top of this tree. Something like a nest? Close to the trunk, where the two crooked branches are. You see it?*

Kurt shaded his eyes and stared upward. The tree was a pine of the genus Araucariaceae, a type rare in the outside world. Kurt had heard that such trees now grew only in Australia and New Zealand. They were fairly common in Dinotopia, though. This specimen was about thirty feet tall, with thickly clustered branches and spiky dark green needles. It gave off a deep, piny scent, sharp in the morning air.

After straining for some time, Kurt finally caught sight of the "nest," if that's what it was. He didn't think so. It was very untidy for a bird's nest, for one thing, looking more like a bundle of creeper-like shoots. He turned to Tostri. "I think that may be a parasite plant," he said carefully. "Or maybe it's a saprophyte."

Are those healer words? Tostri inquired.

Kurt said, "A parasite feeds on its host. A sapro-phyte doesn't. It just—perches on the host, without taking anything from it. Anyway, that plant is new to me. I'll climb up and get a sample."

Be careful, Tostri signed. He ran the tip of his tongue over his lips, as he sometimes did when anxious. *I am nervous about this place.*

Tostri boosted Kurt to the lower branches of the pine, and then Kurt threaded his way slowly up. The strange bundle of tangled, drooping shoots reminded him a bit of Spanish moss, though its tendrils were thicker and a much darker green. The pine branches clustered thick, and Kurt had to squeeze his way be-tween them. Soon his hands were sticky with sap, and he began to wonder if the plant would be worth the climb.

As Kurt finally got close to the strange clinging plant, he saw with surprise that the tendrils had grown through a skull—another bird's skull. Like spiny vines, the plant's shoots twisted through the empty eye sockets. A single black feather lay tangled in more shoots a little closer to the trunk.

At last Kurt drew level with the plant and saw in its tangled mass more bones. The tendrils had nasty-looking spines, he saw now, short, sharp, inward-curving thorns that could catch and hold the unwary.

Kurt frowned. Could the plant possibly be carnivorous? He had seen some sundews before, plants that captured insects with leaves coated with sticky gum. But sundews grew in swamps and bogs, not in trees. And the largest prey they snared was no larger than a cricket or—

Kurt's attention was yanked from the plant by a burst of white at the edge of his vision. Through the branches of the trees, he saw a huge plume of steam shooting up from Brightfire Mountain. It rose straight, then spread out into a billowing mushroom cloud. The whole mountain trembled. And across the canopy of rainforest flowed a strange arc, like a semi-circular wind bowing the trees before it—

A shock wave! Kurt had barely realized it before he felt the thrashing of an earth tremor. He slipped, grabbed wildly for a hold, and felt fire scorch his palm.

The sudden pain made him jerk away. He had plunged his hand into the heart of the strange plant, and now half a dozen tendrils had hooked their spines into his flesh. The tree swayed wildly. Below, Kurt saw Tostri leap back, gesturing frantically up at him.

Kurt heard a weird, low-pitched groan and a rattle of stone. As the tree tilted out toward the cliff, Kurt realized that the entire rocky overhang was breaking free! Tons of stone and earth tore loose and slipped down the steep slope. The trees rooted in the earth were carried along!

For an instant, Kurt thought his tree was going to fall completely and be battered to splinters, but somehow it remained upright, riding the mass of earth and stone down the steep ridge like a child sledding on a snowy hill.

Kurt could only cling to the tree. A choking cloud of gray dust rose, and flying pebbles hit him like painful hailstones. The clump of earth and rocks slid down the cliff faster and faster, the tree whipping him left and right. The whole mass toppled forward—

Kurt shouted in alarm as he felt himself catapulted free of the pine. For a few seconds, he tumbled through the air, head over heels and heels over head. Then he plummeted into the thick canopy of the rainforest. Branches caught him, bent, broke. Gasping, choking, Kurt felt them break his fall, slow him down. He grabbed desperately for handholds. All around him, boulders—the size of his head, the size of his torso—crashed through the canopy. His ears filled with thunder as the enormous chunk of soil and trees crashed somewhere nearby.

Then he hit a branch, doubled over it, and fell free. He smashed to earth with a shock that made lights dance in his head. Kurt had landed on his back on a yielding surface. Still, the breath chuffed from his lungs and he lay with his chest heaving, trying to breathe. A pall of fine dust sifted down on him.

After what seemed like forever, air rushed into his lungs again. Coughing and gagging, Kurt staggered to his feet. His ears were roaring, and his knees shook as he tried to stand and get his bearings. Though scratched and bruised, he seemed to be in one piece.

His right hand throbbed painfully. The thorny tendrils of the strange plant had hooked themselves well into his flesh, and he had torn half a dozen of them free when he went flying from the tree. Kurt gingerly unhooked the thorns. He slipped the tendrils into his collection pouch, although he discovered that, for some reason, he was moving in slow motion.

Then a dull rushing sound filled his ears. At first he thought the rockslide was continuing. No rocks fell, yet the noise grew louder. *Inside my head!* he thought. *I must be hurt.* His eyes wouldn't stay focused. Kurt dimly saw that his hand was swollen. His fingers were puffy sausages, with dozens of tiny puncture wounds oozing blood. *Did I hit my head?* he wondered. No, he didn't think so. He had been jolted, but all his scratches and abrasions were on his arms, chest, and legs. *I must have—have—what's wrong with me? I can't, can't find the words—*

Kurt's lungs were pumping hard, but the air around him seemed thick. He tried to focus his eyes on his swollen hand. *The plant! It traps birds and animals by poison!* A wave of dizziness made him stumble. *Have to get back up,* he thought. *Have, have to climb the, climb the—what? Father at the top. Healer. Need help—*

His legs would not obey him. He fell against a tree, then slipped to the ground. Air whistled in his throat. *Swelling!* he thought. In his mind, he saw a skull, a small skull pierced with the plant's tendrils. How potent was the poison? Could it kill a large animal? *Could it kill me?*

Kurt lurched upward, fighting panic. A murky purple mist had formed, hiding the world. He tried to shout for help and heard himself croak faintly. The world grew completely dark. Kurt's head spun. He could feel his pulse pounding in his temples, hammer blows inside his head. As if his feet were weighed down with lead, Kurt took a single uncertain step forward, another one, and then fell.

He was unconscious before he hit the rainforest floor.

CHAPTER 3

Tostri sensed something wrong a heartbeat before the tremor hit. The hint came through his toes, as a long, shuddering vibration, and it set off an immediate alarm in his mind. He did not know what the trouble was, but his every nerve screamed out *Warning!*

With all the instincts of a predator, he stiffened and whipped his head from side to side, glaring around for the source of danger. In that moment, the vibration became a tremor. Although he could hear nothing, Tostri felt the earth shake. In the same instant, he glimpsed the mushrooming cloud of steam from the distant volcano and understood.

This tremor was much stronger than the one he had felt back in camp. And beneath his feet, the earth *felt* wrong. It was not just shaking, it was breaking to pieces—

Tostri jerked his gaze upward. In the tree above him, Kurt clung to a branch and stared down in shock. Tostri signed urgently: *Jump down!*

But before he had even finished, the ground below

his feet bucked and heaved like the deck of a ship in a hurricane. With a shuddering lurch, the lip of the cliff toppled forward, taking four trees with it. A jagged crack opened right at Tostri's feet. Instinctively, he leaped backward.

In the gap, tree roots parted, sending puffs of dust and sprays of sap flying. A portion of the overhang six strides deep and eight wide broke completely free and slid down the steep slope, a storm of dust and boulders bursting down with it.

Tostri teetered on the brink of a steep drop, fighting for balance. He stared down, horrified, at the accelerating mass of earth, stones, and trees. In the middle of it all was Kurt, clinging to the pine branches, his face pale against the silent, swirling billows of dust. Before the rockslide had even struck the forest below the ridge, Tostri leaped to the right, desperately trying to find some way down.

It was hopeless, and for a moment Tostri stood there, uncertain of what to do. Even balanced at the verge of the cliff, he could not clearly see what had become of his friend. A thin gray river of soil and pebbles still flowed down the slope like a dry waterfall. Below, the roiling clouds of dust hid everything. Tostri could make out nothing for certain. His heart beat fast with alarm for his friend.

But at least he had the impression that the tree Kurt had been in had not been ground to splinters. As far as Tostri had seen, the pine had not fallen over, nor had Kurt toppled out of it. If only Kurt had been able to hold on . . .

Tostri knew he had to find some way down to his friend, and fast. Kurt could be hurt or dazed. He certainly would be shaken.

But Tostri quickly saw that after the rockslide, the slope here was too steep for him to attempt to climb down. Perhaps farther back along the ridge it might be possible, though. As the dust settled, he craned to see if he could catch a glimpse of Kurt, but the forest canopy had swallowed everything.

A thought struck Tostri: *What of Stanhope Ramos?* Had the campsite toppled during the shock?

With an involuntary hiss of concern, Tostri ran back toward camp. He felt reassured when the *Cloudclimber* came into view. His long legs carried him in great striding leaps. Stanhope Ramos would help. Together they would go after Kurt.

The healer met him two-thirds of the way. "Tostri!" he said, his human expression one of alarm. "Are you all right? Where is Kurt?"

Tostri signed quickly, telling the healer that Kurt had fallen. *We must try to climb down,* he ended. *We should do it here. The cliff is steeper farther along the ridge.*

The healer nodded his agreement, his black beard bobbing. "I'll get ropes!"

As Stanhope Ramos rushed back toward camp, Tostri began to descend. The slope was difficult, but he could scramble down. And rocky outcrops, narrow ledges across the face of the ridge, gave him resting places. He had climbed nearly thirty strides—about a hundred and seventy feet, in human terms—when a rope snaked down nearby.

Tostri immediately grasped and held it while Stanhope slid down. As soon as he had joined the dinosaur on a narrow ledge of stone, Stanhope uncoiled a second rope from his shoulder. He held it out and said, "If you can hold my weight, lower me to the next ledge. Then you can come."

I can hold your weight, Tostri replied. He took a couple of turns of rope around his waist and leaned back as Stanhope slipped over the edge. He held on until, far below, Stanhope found a foothold. As soon as he felt the rope slacken, Tostri looked below. Stanhope stood safe on the last and widest ledge. Tostri answered his wave and dropped the end of the rope. Then he leaped to a lower stone outcrop, bounded from that one to a wide one still lower, and then reversed direction, finally coming to rest next to the father of his human friend.

Stanhope's face was red with exertion and taut with strain. He visibly forced a smile onto his face and said, "You're like a mountain goat."

I am like a mountain dinosaur, Tostri corrected. *I only hope we can get up again when we find Kurt. No more ledges below us. What now?*

They were still a hundred feet up the side of Rugged Ridge. Stanhope gestured toward the slope to their right. "I think there's an easier path down." They sidled along the ledge until they came to a dry wash that zigzagged downward. Stanhope quickly looped the coil of rope over his shoulder. "I think I can scramble down without too much risk. Can you make it?"

Tostri studied the wash. Then he gave an almost human nod, that useful gesture of agreement. *Let me go first. If you fall into me, I might be able to stop you. But if I fell against you, we would both be in trouble.*

Tostri knew that the descent would be easier for Stanhope than for himself. He started down, gathering speed. The wash was only a few strides across, and by bounding from one wall to the other, Tostri kept his descent more or less under control. Behind Tostri, Stanhope hurried along, occasionally slipping, sending bursts of pebbles bounding down the gradient.

Finally, they reached the bottom of the ridge. For a few hundred strides, the land was bare gray rock, ancient solidified lava, and then the vegetation began. Tostri's nostrils flared. Even at this distance, the rainforest smelled strongly of growth and life: burgeoning plants, flowing water, birds, small mammals, amphibians, reptiles.

Stanhope turned toward Tostri and said, "Which way?"

31

Tostri took the lead. They skirted the base of the ridge as far as they could, to a spot where the rockfall had made the lava apron impassable. They could see the jumbled boulders and even one of the pines many strides away, in the forest itself. For a few strides, they fought their way through thick underbrush and heavy growths of cycads, short palmetto-like plants with bayonet-shaped leaves. Then they plunged into the shade of the forest. After a few more strides, they walked on a springy surface of old fallen trees and decaying vegetation. The true rainforest trees grew such a dense canopy that the surface, deprived of sunlight, could support few competing plants. They hurried along in a green gloom, humid and almost windless.

All Tostri's attention was focused on the rockslide. How long had it taken him to run toward the camp, to climb down the ridge? Probably two hours or a little less, though it seemed an age to him. Ahead, Tostri saw a shaft of sunlight, then a scatter of boulders. Broken tree branches reeked of pine sap, and a thin, dry hint of dust still hung in the humid air. Tostri pointed to the jumble of rock and tree branches. *There. Kurt will be there.*

Stanhope passed him. As Tostri followed the healer, he blinked at what he saw. Incredibly, the semi-circular chunk of earth and stone that had slipped down the cliff lay reasonably intact. The trees rooted in it had crashed forward, three of them broken short at about the height of a man's head. The fourth tree, the one Kurt had perched in, had caught in the canopy of the rainforest and leaned forward at a steep angle.

Tostri saw Stanhope cup his hand to his mouth. He realized that the healer was probably shouting Kurt's name. But from the stricken expression on Stanhope's face, he must have received no answer. Tostri passed him and prowled over the fallen stone, looking for any sign of his friend.

Could Kurt have been buried in the chaos of boulders that had fallen in the slide? Not likely, Tostri decided, because the trees had fallen on top of the stones. Kurt had been poised high up in the one unbroken pine. It was still rooted in the clump of earth, and unless he had fallen—

But what if he *had* fallen or leaped before the slide had crashed to earth? Was he caught in the branches of the forest canopy? Leaning back, Tostri stared upward. Holes in the canopy, spots where boulders had crashed through, let in columns of sunlight. Still, nowhere could Tostri find any sign of Kurt.

That left his sense of smell. It had served his predatory ancestors well in tracking their prey. And even a civilized Deinonychus still had a much sharper nose than a human. Now Tostri cast about in expanding circles from the slide, head low, nostrils twitching, trying to catch Kurt's scent. He knew it well enough—they had been friends for two years now.

But it was Stanhope who first found a clue. From

a dozen strides away, he waved and beckoned, and Tostri hurried over. "Is that a strip of cloth?" Stanhope asked, pointing to a broken branch high overhead. Something tan had caught on the jagged end. In a faint breath of air, it fluttered there. Tostri recognized it at once as a strip ripped from Kurt's shirt. He nodded emphatically, then hurried to a fallen pile of old branches and decomposing leaves near the base of the tree trunk. Something had crushed them down. They still bore the imprint from it, and the depression was the right size for Kurt's body.

Tostri's nostrils told him at once that the "something" had indeed been Kurt. There was a bit of blood, too. Only a little. Perhaps it had come from minor scratches or cuts. The injury surely could be nothing fatal. Tostri whirled and signed, *Kurt was here. He must have fallen when the rockslide reached the forest floor.*

"What's become of him?" Stanhope asked, his expression tight with worry.

Tostri sniffed. He wrinkled his lip in bewilderment. He had found traces of Kurt's trail, yes, quite clear, and reasonably recent. Certainly, Kurt had lain here for a few minutes, then had moved away under his own power. Tostri found no hint of another presence, human or dinosaur. Nothing had attacked the young human; nothing had dragged him away. If he had to guess, Tostri would have judged that Kurt had walked away from this spot no more than an hour ago.

Yet—

Stanhope touched his arm, and when he looked around, the healer asked, "Where is he?"

Tostri signed thoughtfully, *Kurt survived the fall. I think he was not badly hurt. At least I know he was well enough to walk. He lay here for a little while, then left. This is the strange part, though. He seems to have headed away from the ridge.*

"What?" Stanhope peered past Tostri, into the dim reaches of the rainforest. A dark spot appeared on his shoulder. Moisture, collecting on the undersides of the leaves fifty feet overhead, was falling like a slow rain. Tostri felt a drop strike him on the head, and another on his back.

Tostri signed, *I do not understand, either. Kurt is not heading back to the ridge. For some reason, he is going deeper into the forest.*

Stanhope shook his head. His dark beard gleamed in the dim green light. "That's dangerous!"

With a nod, Tostri replied, *Very dangerous, especially if he is hurt. That is why we must hurry. We have to find him before anything else does.*

"Let's go," Stanhope said at once, and they plunged into the unknown depths of the forest.

CHAPTER 4

Kurt staggered through a forest in which the trunks of trees rose and vanished into a purple haze. The darkness around him was more than the shade of a forest canopy, he knew, but he could not wipe the strangeness from his eyes. And his left hand throbbed with pain. All along the palm he'd discovered angry red welts. Dried brownish red splotches of blood showed where eleven curved thorns were lodged beneath his skin. He had no idea how they had gotten there.

But the pain was not as great as his thirst. His throat screamed for water; his tongue felt swollen and rough. Someone, a bearded man, had taught him about finding drink in the wilderness. Water would lie at the bottom of a descending slope. Streams flowed in beds; water collected in lakes and pools. It would be downhill. Somewhere downhill.

Kurt leaned against a tree trunk, panting for breath. His heart was pounding, and the breath rattled harshly in his throat. His thoughts boiled away, like bees swarming from an overset hive. He shook his head, then pushed away from the tree, following the slope of the land.

For an unknown time, Kurt trudged downhill, following the grade. Dimly, he saw a picture of himself standing in a high place, seeing a distant mountain, and a forest cut by silvery ribbons of river. Somewhere ahead he could drink.

Screams of birds sent jolts through his muscles. They seemed far too loud. All around him were scrapes, crackles, and slithery rustles. The noises even came from underfoot, for the surface beneath his feet was more like a springy bed of tangled branches and leaves than earth. Small creatures scuttled through the openings, startling him and making him want to run.

He came to a patch of sunlight, brighter than the violet shadow of the forest. A broken trunk lay across Kurt's path. Through the hole it had ripped in the canopy above, Kurt could see a patch of blue sky. Lianas, tropical vines, hung down, their ends snapped and turning brown in the moist air. Kurt reached the fallen tree. It was a giant, easily a hundred feet long. Not wanting to go around, he clambered over the fallen trunk and heard a hiss.

He looked fearfully to his left. A—what was it called? Long animal, legless, scaled skin that was leaf brown splotched with yellow—*snake!* A snake was within a yard of his face. Its heavy body lay looped around a branch of the fallen tree. The sight of it made Kurt's bones feel like ice. As Kurt watched, frozen, the snake's triangular head suddenly reared.

With a hoarse shout, Kurt leaped forward, off the trunk. His left foot plunged into a gap in the ancient tree branches on the forest floor. He felt the rotten wood clutch his ankle, giving it a painful wrench. Still yelling, Kurt tugged his foot free and ran limping away from the threat.

Part of his mind fought the fear. Not big enough. Harmless. Not poisonous. But none of the thoughts had any power. The snake was behind him, and so he ran. He ran without thought, without reason.

Once as he flailed through another fallen tree crown, a branch snagged him. Kurt struggled against it. He discovered that a branch had caught on something he wore on a strap, a leather pouch. For a moment, Kurt was ready to let it go, to drop it just to get away, but something made him hang on. He snapped the branch and freed the strap. He found he could thrust his wounded hand through the strap, rest it on the pouch, and find a little relief. He blundered on.

Twice he rested briefly, but he could not really stand to pause for very long. A tree toad booming out its mating call, a writhing foot-long orange-and-black centipede hastening past at his feet—they were all terrifying.

All the while, his thirst grew. It became the one reality in his world. He had to find water. His body raged for water. Maddeningly, drops of it fell on him, body-warm and pelting after their fall from the canopy above. But a drop of water splashing on his face or his shoulder did Kurt no good.

Stumbling on, Kurt saw a blaze of sunlight through the trees. A huge dragonfly, its wingspan easily nine inches, droned past. He limped onward, pushing through a dense mat of reeds. Suddenly, he was aware that he was standing in the sun, lost in a thicket of reeds taller than he was. Mud sucked at his feet with each step he took.

Mud!

Kurt recognized what that meant. He could ease his thirst somewhere nearby. If only he could see. Using his good right hand, Kurt shoved his way through the reeds, so thick that they were all but impassable. His foot slipped on a hard surface. Rock, not mud. He lunged against the wall of reeds and tumbled forward on hands and knees. He landed painfully, the shock sending a jolt through his injured left hand.

But he landed on a broad, flat gray rock. Ahead was a stretch of black sand, glittering in the noon sun, and past that was—

Water.

A river gurgled over a stone bed, thirty feet across here. It had looped, and here in the inner curve of the loop, the wide sandy shore had piled up. To Kurt's right was a broad expanse, its surface streaked with foam from the rocks. He rose, staggered, fell on the sand, and half-crawled to the edge of the water.

Burying his face in the coolness, he drank deeply.

His swollen tongue seemed to shrink to its proper size. When at last his thirst was better, Kurt plunged his sore left hand into the soothing water. After a few minutes, he pulled it out and looked at the palm. The blunt ends of some thorns were almost at the surface of his skin. Using his teeth, he pulled out as many as he could, spitting them aside.

A few, three or four, were buried too deeply to remove. Kurt dragged himself back to the edge of the reeds, where the tall plants leaned forward over the rock and gave some shade. Huddled there, he closed his eyes. He slept.

When he came to again, the sun was lower. A breeze had sprung up, rattling the reeds. The sky overhead hurried with clouds, puffy cumulus against a higher layer of wispy cirrus. Kurt gingerly stood up. He could keep his balance, and perhaps his hand was a little less swollen.

But other than that, he knew almost nothing. He had a vague impression of a fall, of an eternity of thirst. Aside from that, he could not recall even his own name. He knew only that he was alone, that he needed to drink again, and that he was in danger. What kind of danger he could not say.

He crawled to the river and bent to drink again. As he did, the leather pouch slipped on its strap and fell into the water. Kurt yanked it back, feeling protective of it. When he had satisfied his thirst, he opened the leather pouch, stared at the strands of plant inside, and closed it again. Keep this? Yes, he must. That seemed very important. Keep it.

Kurt shook his head. He sat motionless, hunkered on the black sand at the edge of the stream, hearing the water splash over stone, hearing the drone of dragonflies as they patrolled the air near the reeds.

Movement attracted his gaze. Kurt held his breath. Something was moving in the reeds a few steps from him.

He made out a dark shape, a long neck, long legs—and then the creature stepped to the edge of the pool. It tilted its head, and its bright eye gleamed as it took him in. Then, cautiously, it took three more steps. It was a—bird?—yes, a bird, a wading bird.

Kurt frowned. He had seen this sort of creature before, though he couldn't think where. He felt that it would not hurt him. As he watched, the bird stabbed a long beak into the water, came up with a thrashing, silvery minnow, and gobbled it down. It shook itself, drops of water flying from its head in a silvery spray. Then it gave a creaking call.

Three others joined it. They waded into the river, making their way slowly across the stream to the opposite bank. Their feathers were a deep brown, dappled with white and black. Their necks were long and snakelike, their eyes a glittering black, rimmed with white. The four birds snatched fish and crayfish from the stream bed. Kurt could see that the river was not very deep, no more than waist-high on him. The smallest of the birds ducked completely under the surface once and came up with a writhing eel clutched in its beak.

"Ic—" Kurt croaked softly to himself. The sound of his own voice startled him. His face twisted in an effort to remember, but it failed. He could not think of the rest of the word, the name for this creature.

He watched the birds as they emerged on the far bank, wading at the very edge of the river. Two of them squabbled over some morsel that one had turned up from the shelter of a stone. Past them a stand of reeds stretched away, and beyond the reeds a belt of cycads, and then the rainforest again—

Thunder grumbled from somewhere far away. A moment later, the earth trembled. Kurt closed his eyes. As if he were seeing a picture on the inside of his eyelids, he had a quick vision: a conical mountain, leaping with fire, spraying out a billow of steam. He opened his eyes again.

And saw the reeds stir in sudden movement.

Reptilian creatures, standing on their hind legs, had melted from the reedbed. They wore leather headbands with reeds worked into them. Their forelegs ended in three-taloned hands, and in these hands, they clutched spears. Kurt felt his heart thud again. These creatures were taller than he was, much taller. But they did not seem to have noticed him. They moved to keep a clump of tall reeds between them and the birds.

As the largest of the birds stalked past the creatures, two of them leaped out with high-pitched shouts. The birds panicked. Three of them took to the air and flew upstream. The last one, cut off from its group, squawked in alarm and darted for the cover of the reeds. The two dinosaurs still in the reedbed raised their spears and dashed toward the bird, while the two in the river closed behind it. They all vanished into the reeds.

A moment later, Kurt heard a rattle of reeds and a shriek, cut short.

They had killed it!

A sense of wrongness flooded Kurt. No one killed! It was unheard of! He leaped to his feet—

And saw, across the stream, a fifth dinosaur. It had stood so motionless that his gaze had passed right over it.

It carried no spear. But it saw Kurt, and it straightened in obvious surprise. The dinosaur splashed out into the water, coming halfway across the stream. Then, suddenly, it thrust out both its hands, its three claws clenched into fists.

With an inarticulate cry, Kurt ran. Not back into the forest, for the reeds blocked his path, and he had a confused notion that the dinosaurs might trap him as they had trapped the bird. Kurt ran for his life, splashing through the water along the edge of the stream, following its path downriver. And he picked up speed when, behind him, he heard a burst of shrill hoots.

The hunters were calling to each other!

CHAPTER 5

Kurt ran until he could hardly feel his legs, and then he stumbled on. To his right, the river grew choppier, spumed into white foam, roared over rocks. At some point, it turned into white water, thundering in his ears. Spray leaped from a million hidden rocks, drifted on a faint breeze, soaked him.

Still, he ran.

He kept glimpsing the bird hunters on the opposite shore, their long legs carrying them easily. They paced him, chattering, gesturing. *Danger!* screamed Kurt's instincts.

And yet—

Some part of his mind, buried beneath layers of fear, wanted him to stop. Some remote memory struggled to awaken. An image of another Deinonychus drifted somewhere behind his eyes, a creature with intelligence and compassion . . .

The shoreline grew steeper, rockier. Kurt had worked his way from the water to the shore, but now the rocks forced him back into the edge of the stream, and he waded, the water dragging at his ankles. He turned. His two pursuers were farther back. They held up their fists again as he watched, and he turned and hurried on.

Beneath his feet, the river stones were smooth, treacherous. Eons of running water had ground them to roundness, to apple or pumpkin-sized balls. Dark brownish green algae had covered them, made them slick. Every step among such stones balanced fear with skill, but every step took him downstream from the two dinosaurs on the opposite shore. He passed a low island, its upstream end piled high with driftwood, which concealed him from the dinosaurs. For a moment, he paused, gasping for breath.

Kurt saw that the opposite bank of the river was becoming steeper, too. It had turned into a bluff of black and gray volcanic stone, jumbled, chaotic. The river had cut into it, making a cliff higher than Kurt's head. Not far downstream, the cliff rose to thirty or forty feet. The river took a hard bend to the right there, around a dark volcanic headland. At this point in its course, the snarling stream was too rapid for the hunting dinosaurs to cross. They would have to go far upstream to wade safely.

And the rising cliff on the opposite shore meant they could not pace him. They would have to pull far back into the forest if they tried to follow him on that side.

Safety.

But safety at a price. On Kurt's side of the river, too, the stream edge had become rocky. The bluff on this side wasn't nearly as high, only four or five feet, but the water was halfway up Kurt's calves. And even bracing against the low cliff, Kurt could hardly keep his footing in the rush of water. He would have a hard time clambering ashore, especially with his injured hand.

His breath ripped through his chest in fiery bursts. His hand throbbed. The cold water numbed his legs. Still, he found the strength to flounder on. As he had done in bad dreams, Kurt lifted one heavy foot and placed it in front of the other, then again and again, without seeming to make progress.

Until he was at the bend of the river, with a jagged black cliff rearing off to his right. And before him—

Waterfalls.

No, not quite. Cascades. The river plunged down a long hill, leaping in layers of foamy spray. The cascades continued as far downstream as Kurt could see. The drop was steep. Kurt sensed that he could not keep his balance. He would have to climb out.

The bank to his left came to his chest. He threw his arms over it and tried to hoist himself up. His head spun, and the sunlight faded to that intense violet color. For a moment, he couldn't hear or see, could only sense the drag of the river on his legs. He gasped for air.

He had to climb out. He had to. As his vision

slowly cleared, Kurt ground his teeth together. He put his weight on his elbows and leaped up. He wormed up onto a mossy ledge, his dripping feet projecting over the stream. Before him the forest spread out on either side. Behind him the river screamed as it shot over the cascades.

Then something moved in the shadow of the forest. Kurt caught his breath. Only a hundred yards away, a *shape* rose, towering above the brushy growth. It was a scaly, mottled green. The creature stood on two legs. Its front limbs ended in wickedly curved claws, like huge hooks. And its head was that of a gigantic crocodile, yellowed teeth grinning. The creature's eyes gleamed a dark brown. They focused on Kurt, and with lightning speed, the enormous animal raced toward him.

With a wordless yell, Kurt threw himself back. He landed in the water with a splash and struggled up, only to feel the current snatch his feet from under him. Cold water filled his eyes, stung his nose. He breathed foam, coughed, sank, and saw the world tumble past, sunlight and shadow.

The strap of his pouch caught on a log jammed among the rocks at the edge of the first cascade. He felt the material begin to tear. Desperately, Kurt grabbed for his pouch. The strap gave way—

And Kurt flipped backward, toppling, falling. He was over the edge of the cascade, rushing water all around. He struck the rocky bottom hard, numbing his left shoulder. Now he was spinning underwater with the roar of the river filling his ears, jarring his bones. He crashed into more stones, spun away, rose to the surface, gasped air, fell again. He could not attempt to swim. He couldn't even be sure where the surface was. He hit the next cascade, went over feet-first, as if he were riding a long slide, gasped air, and then hit the next one.

The river was either going to drown him or batter him to death. Kurt could only rear his head, snatch a breath of air, and try to ride the current without smashing against a rock. How long he hurtled through the rush of water, he did not know. His only impressions were speed, cold, and the struggle to breathe.

Then he was in midair, falling. Water broke his fall, and he rolled over and over until finally his head came up again, and with a long, burning breath, he found himself miles from the top of the cascades, in the pool the last waterfall had carved into the stone. He was near the shore. A black beach curved in a crescent there. Kurt crawled out on hands and knees.

No bones seemed to be broken, though he was badly bruised and bleeding from a dozen scrapes and scratches. His fingers found a nasty lump over his left ear. He coughed up a quart of river water. The memory of the enormous predator made him shiver.

He dragged himself into some brush and saw ahead of him the face of the cliff. A dark, round opening yawned at him. Kurt saw an image in his mind:

molten rock, lava, pouring through an opening like that. Without being able to name it, he somehow understood that the lava tube offered refuge. He crawled to it. The opening was between three and four feet in diameter and led back into darkness.

The huge predator couldn't hope to fit in. The two smaller ones weren't built for the kind of crawling it would take.

Kurt crept inside. The roar of the waterfall faded, became a faint background vibration. He was soaked and cold, and by contrast the smooth stone surface felt warm. Twenty feet in from the opening, Kurt collapsed, unable to drag himself any farther. With a last effort, he turned so he could keep an eye on the mouth of the tunnel, a bright, round window onto a world of green reeds.

That was all he could do. He lay with the smooth stone pressing his stomach and breathed hard. Then, without relaxing, he was suddenly unconscious, drifting in a sleep haunted by images of crocodile-headed monsters.

CHAPTER 6

Well past noon, Tostri smelled water ahead. For a moment, he stood almost on the tips of his toes, trying to catch any vibration, any sign of Kurt nearby. Nothing. And yet, Kurt's scent lingered. He had certainly passed this way, and not long before. Tostri signed to Stanhope: *Kurt came this way. Heading for water, I think.*

Stanhope nodded, his sweating red face grim above the black beard. Tostri took the lead. They stepped from the shade of the forest into cloudy daylight. Now Tostri could feel the faint vibration of running water somewhere very near. He broke a path through the undergrowth and found the bed of reeds, their stems broken and crushed. He pushed his way through and emerged on the edge of the river pool. Tostri narrowed his eyes. There were marks in the black sand—footprints of birds, and scuffs that might have been left by a human foot. His nostrils flared as he read the complicated mix of scents.

Kurt's was there, fading but still clear. And he had been right about the birds. He could smell four of them, probably Ichthyornis. This was the kind of territory they liked. And—a deep sniff—Deinonychus, too, more than one, their distinctive traces mingled with the unfamiliar scent of leather. Tostri signed, *Wait*. Then he cast about on the shore of the pool. He could find traces of Kurt's scent along the beach, but it led only to the water. For some minutes, Tostri tried to pick up the scent upstream and downstream, but he could find nothing. Kurt must have gone into the water.

Or perhaps he had crossed. The pool was seven or eight strides wide, but it did not look deep. Tostri plunged into the water, feeling the grainy black sand beneath his toes, sensing that downstream from here, the river picked up speed, that upstream it was a slower, lazier watercourse.

Tostri emerged on the far bank, where, to his immediate alarm, he smelled the sharp reek of blood. Not human, though—one of the birds, perhaps. He remembered the reports that had come back to Dinotopia about the tribes on Outer Island. They were hunters, each tribe semi-independent of all the others. And the hunters had built up a complex social organization. Their values were not those of the deinonychids who had chosen the high civilization of Dinotopia, yet—

Through his toes, Tostri sensed the vibration of someone's footsteps close behind him—human, not dinosaur. He whirled to discover that Stanhope had followed him. "Where is Kurt?" he asked.

Before Tostri could even begin to sign a reply, shapes emerged from the shadows of the trees. Deinonychids, half a dozen of them. Tostri could only sign, *Don't alarm them* before the strange dinosaurs had surrounded Tostri and Stanhope. They were all talking at once, and Tostri could not follow what they said. As always, he had more difficulty reading dinosaur speech than human speech. Deinonychid lips did not move much, but usually Tostri could work out the gist of the words by observing the movement of dinosaur tongues and eyes. Not this time. He could not make out a syllable. He signed, *Friends. We are friends.*

Two of the deinonychids looked at each other. Then they gave Tostri a flurry of gesture-signals that looked familiar but made no sense. They were like a jumble of unrelated words: *sky, fire, small, see, run.* He signed for them to go more slowly, but they didn't seem to understand him, either. They gabbled at each other, one of them repeatedly gesturing toward the rainforest.

Stanhope said to Tostri, "Their dialect is very different from the way deinonychids speak on Dinotopia. I'm not sure I can understand any of it, but I'll try to speak to them." Stanhope turned away, and Tostri had to move to read his friend's lips as Stanhope was saying, ". . . seeking a boy, lost and perhaps hurt. A young human."

The deinonychids did not seem to understand. One of them pointed again, indicating the forest. The strange dinosaur made sharp gestures, as if trying to warn the newcomers—*Or perhaps,* Tostri thought, *to frighten us.*

For a moment, they all stood staring at each other.

Then a figure came out from the shadows of the trees. The dinosaurs took a step back, and the new one, crowned with a leather cap adorned with red and green feathers, came through the crowd and spoke to Stanhope.

Stanhope exchanged some words with him, then turned to Tostri and said, "This one speaks a little of a dialect I recognize. He says his name is Eklok and that he is the leader of the Bird Tribe. He says we are in the tribe's territory, and that is forbidden."

Tostri replied, *Tell Eklok our names. Apologize. Explain we are looking for a—say a lost yearling.*

Stanhope spread his hands, palms up, in a Dinotopian gesture of apology. In his rough human approximation of deinonychid speech, he said, "We are sorry, Hunter Eklok. We apologize for our intrusion. I am Stanhope Ramos, a healer. My friend here is Tostri, son of Etros and Etarah. We did not mean to violate your territory. We seek my son, a young one, a yearling of our—our tribe. He is lost and hurt."

Tostri watched impatiently as Eklok responded in a long speech punctuated with gestures that he could not clearly comprehend. Stanhope finally shook his head. "His dialect is very hard to follow. He seems to be saying that a boy was here, but fled. He wants us to come with him into the forest, I think."

Eklok turned and chattered at Tostri. Stanhope spoke for him: "Eklok, Tostri cannot hear. He cannot speak."

Eklok's eyes widened in surprise. He tilted his head and said something else. Tostri responded by very simple sign language: *I cannot hear your words. I can speak with talking claws.* He held out his hands, his claws balled into fists. It was an ancient gesture of his kind, an offer of friendship or at least of truce. Closed claws could not fight.

Slowly, Eklok extended his hands, then clenched his claws into fists, too. With a deliberate simplicity, he pointed first to Tostri, then to Stanhope. He gestured toward the rainforest and made a circular motion. Tostri realized that the hunter was offering a truce—but he was insisting that Tostri and Stanhope come with them into the rainforest.

"What about Kurt?" Stanhope insisted, his forehead furrowed into a worried frown.

Tostri tilted his head and considered. *I think we should go with the hunters. They have many searchers and we are only two. And what is more important, they are hunters by nature. If they will help, we will find Kurt much more quickly.*

Stanhope did not look pleased. "I don't like their ordering us into their camp. They could hold us for as long as they wanted, and meanwhile Kurt is somewhere out here."

Tostri agreed: *That is possible, but I do not think likely. Eklok does not seem threatening. Just insistent.* He did not add that they had very little choice. The hunters outnumbered them and, if they wished, could simply force Tostri and Stanhope to come with them.

With Eklok leading and the other hunters bringing up the rear, Stanhope and Tostri climbed the slope through the undergrowth. Before long they came into a clearing where a low, almost smokeless fire burned. Surrounding it were temporary shelters, hutlike structures of saplings and woven reeds. Hanging on simple wooden frames near the fire, drying in the heat, were long strips of meat.

Eklok offered some of this to Tostri, who refused by turning his head, an old gesture among deinonychids that meant "No thank you." Then, with some false starts and many pauses for thought, the two of them began to work out a gesture language that they could both understand. It didn't take long before Tostri realized why the deinonychids' gestures had looked so familiar—their gestures were a rudimentary form of the gestures Tostri himself had been taught long ago.

How do you live? Eklok was demanding. *A hunter must have keen hearing. How do you sense threats? How do you sense prey?*

Tostri found himself puzzled. The questions were

open, but behind them lay some strange feeling. Was it resentment? He signed, *I am not without senses. After all, I have my eyes, my sense of smell. And I am not a hunter. At home I help my friends in study.*

Eklok could not understand the word *study*. Perhaps he knew what *reading* was—Tostri had learned that hunters often left messages in soft earth or mud for the rest of their tribe—but he did not know about scrolls or of libraries. Nothing Tostri could do clarified the idea for him, and at last he jerked his head upward in an expression of impatience. *I know nothing of these things. What good is a hunter who cannot hunt?* he signed.

This time, Tostri caught a definite undertone of contempt and resentment. He realized that, to Eklok, all deinonychids were hunters. Any of his kind who could not hunt was worthless. To Tostri, used to the acceptance of all differences in Dinotopia, Eklok's attitude was surprising.

Tostri carefully replied, *On the large island, we have our own ways. They are different from yours. I am not a hunter among my people. But your people are great hunters. We need hunters to help us find my lost friend. We ask your aid.*

Eklok summoned others of his tribe to him. They stepped aside and began to talk among themselves.

"I think I caught most of that," Stanhope said to Tostri. "Although their gestures are almost as strange to me as their dialect." He stroked his thick beard. His eyes were worried. "Tostri, if they won't help us, we have to go, and soon. Kurt could be in trouble."

Eklok returned. He spoke, and Stanhope listened gravely. Then he translated for Tostri. "Eklok says they asked us back to the camp for our own safety. He says something about a large danger or great danger on the other side of the river. If we want to find Kurt, Eklok's hunters will help us, despite this danger, but . . ."

Here, Stanhope listened to Eklok again. He turned back to Tostri, looking troubled.

"But they will help only if you prove you are a hunter!"

CHAPTER 7

Tostri looked on as Stanhope tried one last time to explain. "Eklok, you must understand. In Dinotopia your kinsmen are not hunters. Tostri is the son of Etros and Etarah. They live in a great city. Etros is a teacher, a much-respected writer of scrolls. Etarah is an artist, a musician. Their son has never hunted or—"

Eklok jerked his head to the side: *No, I do not accept this.* Then he said something and gestured toward Tostri.

Stanhope nodded. "Yes, his name is an unusual one for a Deinonychus. It means 'the silent one,' as it does in your speech. However, in Dinotopia the word has taken on more meaning. It can also mean 'the thinker,' or 'the one who contemplates.' To us, to all of Tostri's family and friends, his name is not a term of weakness but of strength."

Tostri felt more and more anxious. Time was passing. Here under the canopy of the forest, Tostri could not see the sky, but he could sense that the sun had vanished behind clouds. Somewhere up there, a thin rain fell, but under the trees, only a drop plummeted to earth here and there. Was Kurt somewhere out in the rain, exposed to the elements?

Eklok conferred with two of his hunters for a few moments before turning again. To Tostri, Eklok signed, *We are losing hunting time. Give your decision now. Will you prove you are a hunter?*

Tostri bowed his head. With unusual sharpness, he felt everything around him: the scent of the slow fire, the small vibration of the rain on the leaves high overhead, the hard light in Eklok's eyes. Tostri considered for a moment, then signed, *I will not kill.*

Eklok thought about that. *But if we ask you merely to stalk, how will you show that you have skill? How will you show that one who does not hear can hunt?*

Tostri signed, *I am willing to try, but the yearling is lost! He is hurt! Whatever you want me to do, we must do it quickly!*

Eklok considered. *You are almost an adult. Even in Dinotopia, you must be beyond the age of playing. Still, children's games can help prepare us to be adults. Here the children of the tribe have a hunting game that may serve as a test of your ability. Wait.* He turned and gave a cry. Tostri could not hear the sound, of course, but from Eklok's expression, he thought the chieftain might have snapped out some kind of order to his followers.

"Tostri," Stanhope said, "we had better just go back. It's getting dark. A storm may be brewing, and if Kurt—"

Tostri shook his head, a human gesture. *I am worried about this danger Eklok keeps hinting at. We may need Eklok's help to deal with it. Let me try his game.*

A young hunter, his face painted with yellow and red streaks of earth, loped into the clearing and stood as Eklok spoke to him. Tostri could not follow the rapid exchange of speech at all, though at one point the newcomer gave him a long, quizzical look. Then Eklok turned back to Tostri and began to sign. *This is the youngest hunter among us. He is about your age, I think. He is*— Eklok broke off, finding no way to sign the name. He said something to Stanhope.

Stanhope passed the young hunter's name to Tostri: "He says this is Edon."

Tostri nodded. Edon, helped by two others, was strapping himself into an extraordinary suit of body armor. It looked as if it were made of a thick, corklike bark, the pieces held together by rawhide thongs. Tostri's nostrils twitched. The bark had a pungent smell, sharp and strong.

Eklok signed, *My hunter will go into the brush. You must track him down. You must do it before sunset. If you can track him and take a token from him, then you are a hunter. You will have our respect, and we will help you find your lost friend. If you do not succeed in the hunt, you must take your chances alone with the great danger.*

"What is it?" asked Stanhope anxiously. "I can't follow all of his signs. What is he saying?"

Tostri translated. Seeing Stanhope's stricken look,

he added, *I do not know what this great danger is. I do not think Eklok will tell us—yet. But I do know we need Eklok's help.*

Eklok wore a roughly woven neck cloth, dyed a bright red. He removed it and tied it around Edon's neck. Then he gave a sharp nod, and the young hunter dashed away, along a trail that led into the rainforest. In a moment, he had vanished around a bend.

Eklok turned back to Tostri and signed, *Now you will be the hunter. If you find your prey, you must remove the token from his neck and bring it back. That will prove your hunt has been successful. But I warn you that prey can be dangerous. Edon will not give up the token without a struggle. If you can even track him. If you can even find him. We will give him a fair start. Then you must show us your hunting skills.*

Tostri explained the situation to Stanhope, who shook his head, looking more and more worried. Again he tried to make clear to Eklok that Kurt was his son, that he was alone and probably injured.

Eklok listened patiently, but he refused to give in. "We are hunters," he told Stanhope. "The way of the hunter is to survive. If your friend can prove he is a hunter, then he is truly one of us, and we will help. But I do not think he can do it. The forest demands all of a hunter's attention. He must have sharp vision, a keen sense of smell, and acute hearing. A hunter cannot be a *tostri,* a silent one."

Understanding that to gain Eklok's aid he would first have to gain his respect, Tostri took deep breaths. True, he could not hear. No matter, he told himself. Vision, his sense of smell, and his sense of touch would have to serve instead.

Some internal clock must have given Eklok a signal. He turned to Tostri and signaled *Go!*

An instant later, Tostri had plunged into the undergrowth on the fringe of the rainforest.

The hunt had begun.

CHAPTER 8

Kurt struggled through feverish dreams: he was in a misty swamp, its floor stagnant mud. Ancient cypress trees rose on every side, their crooked branches dripping with gray-green Spanish moss. The stifling, humid air hummed with darting dragonflies and mosquitoes that were as long as Kurt's little finger. And behind him somewhere was a gigantic crocodile. He could hear its booming roar. It knew he was in its territory, and it was searching him out. Kurt felt a stabbing desire to run, to get away from the monstrous jaws.

But the mud clung to his feet. Each step cost him an agony of effort, each foot wore pounds of caked mud. He ran in nightmare slow motion, unsure of direction, unsure of anything except for the fact that he was prey. And in the reeds, in the water nearby, he heard stealthy sounds, the sounds of a stalker toying with its victim. The predator was always just out of his vision, but close enough for him to sense its presence, its hunger, its determination to kill—

Kurt woke with a gasp, sitting up in darkness. The world spun around him for a moment, and he wondered where he was. His hand throbbed and felt swollen to twice its normal size. For a panicky second, Kurt could recall nothing, but then he saw the tunnel opening, the green world beyond, and in images he remembered the creatures that had pursued him.

Kurt crawled toward the tunnel mouth and cautiously emerged into the gray light of a cloudy afternoon. He must have slept for more than two hours. A thin drizzle drifted down in lazy silver curtains, making almost no sound. To his left, he heard the thunder of the cascades. Kurt struggled to think. This was the side of the river . . . the side the hunters had been on. Maybe he was far enough away from them to be safe. Maybe not.

Kurt stood, reeling with dizziness. His stomach clenched with hunger. He found his way to the riverside and drank, soaking his painful hand again. He could do nothing about the spines that were still beneath his skin, dark streaks at the center of ugly purple blotches. Some instinct led him to unbutton his shirt and thrust his hand in, using it like a sling. Then he explored the riverbank.

Below the cascades, the river broadened into a wide, calm pool. Trees overhung it, and not far from the shore, Kurt spotted an especially tall tree with glossy, drooping, spear-shaped leaves. He could not remember the word for the tree, but he knew it bore edible fruit. When he got close enough, he saw the branches were heavy with them, green pebbly oval shapes that swayed tantalizingly close.

With his injured hand, Kurt could not hope to climb the tree, but he found a fallen branch and was able to knock one of the lower fruits down. It fell heavily, a football-sized reward for his effort. Kurt picked it up and, clutching it to his chest, returned to the mouth of the tunnel. He sat just inside, out of the drifting rain, and smashed the fruit on the stone floor.

It cracked open. Inside the tough, spiny green rind was a golden yellow flesh that was sweet and refreshing. Kurt ate with a ravenous appetite, but paused from time to time to carefully save the seeds in his collection pouch. He didn't even think about why.

Suddenly, he smiled. He opened his mouth, hesitated, and then croaked out a single word: "Nangka." That was the name of the fruit. As tasty as a mango, but much larger. It looked something like a durian, but lacked the foul scent of that fruit. "Nangka." He had a word again. Not much, one word, but it was something, and just speaking it aloud gave him a sense of accomplishment.

Still, his clearing mind told him that his hand was worse. He wasn't sure how, but he knew the pain had grown.

When he had eaten all he wanted, Kurt lay on his stomach and stared out into the drizzly afternoon. He frowned, seeing pictures in his mind. The animals that had first chased him, the hunters of birds, had been armed. They all carried stone-tipped spears. Perhaps if he had a weapon, a spear like theirs, he could protect himself.

Emerging from his hiding place, Kurt went back to the river. At one point, on the outer curve of the pool, driftwood that had washed over the cascades had piled into a chest-high tangle. He prowled through this until he found an uprooted sapling, twice as tall as he was. The bark had weathered off, but the wood felt dry and sturdy. The root end of the sapling was somewhere under the pile of logs, but he would not need the whole thing.

With his good hand, Kurt tugged and shoved at the small tree until it snapped with a sound like a small explosion. He was left with a six-foot-long stick, its broken end already sharp.

But he could make it better. Taking his find back to the lava tube, Kurt methodically scraped the pointed end against the stone floor. As he worked, Kurt tried to recapture more words. In his mind, he pictured a tall, bearded man. He could not remember the man's name, but the image was clear. More than that, Kurt linked a feeling to the image: this tall, bearded man would protect him, would help him, would heal his injured hand.

Where was he? Kurt's memory was confused, but he had a sense that the man was somewhere upstream from here, at the top of a steep ridge. Other fleeting images came to him, the earth far below, a pale tan gasbag overhead. Flying? Had he somehow been flying?

"Cloudclimber," he said so suddenly that he startled himself. In his mind's eye, Kurt saw a handsome young Skybax rider, had a picture of him soaring into the sky on his partner's back, strong wings outspread, rising ever higher.

But no more words would come. And whatever *Cloudclimber* might be, it was not a Skybax, not any kind of pterosaur. Kurt sensed somehow that the healer would be near this *Cloudclimber,* and that *Cloudclimber* was somewhere far, far behind him.

He tested the point of his spear. It was only wood, but he had produced a rounded, sharp tip. With it he might be able to spear a fish. He could certainly use it to hold off a threat his own size, at least for a short time.

Grimacing as he wormed out of the tunnel opening, Kurt hefted the spear. It wasn't much. He had only one good hand with which to wield it. But it was something.

The last fall of the cascade was ten or twelve feet tall, a boiling mass of water. His side of the river was the bluff side. Dark, rounded stone, ancient hardened lava, loomed over him. Kurt knew that he would have little chance of scaling the cliffs. He would have to wade across the pool and try the far side. The shore was flatter there, and he could climb beside the cataracts. But the far side was also where the huge beast had surprised him.

For a few minutes, Kurt stood staring at the forest across the pool. The leaves drooped and glistened in the slow, misting rain. Birds chattered from the canopy, but no bulking shadow lurked there. He would have to take his chance.

Leaning on his spear, Kurt crossed the river far down from the falls, near the tangle of driftwood. The sand under his feet was firm, the water cool but not cold. It didn't matter that the pool was so deep that he had to swim part of the way across, awkwardly carrying his spear in the crook of his left arm. With the steady, drizzling rain, he was already about as wet as he could get.

He sloshed ashore. The going would be hard even on this side, he saw, but the slope was not impossible. Above all, he wanted to stick close to the river. It was his only guide, and away from it he might quickly become lost.

The way up was slippery and steep, the volcanic rock wet from the spray of the cascades. Kurt had to strain to climb over rounded boulders, helping himself by leaning on his spear or by grasping creepers with his good hand and hauling himself up. Often he had to detour, straying to the fringes of the forest. Always, though, he made his way back to the river.

The sky was sullen, and ragged gray clouds almost brushed the forest canopy on either side of the river.

The constant rain drifted down, soaking him. His sodden tunic seemed to weigh a ton, and his wet shoes began to chafe his heels. From time to time, waves of dizziness washed over him, giving him a panicky feeling.

Yet Kurt didn't slow down. Off to his right, the forest was thick enough to hide anything, even the crocodile-headed predator that had reared suddenly from the darkness. He would have no hope against such a threat.

But somewhere ahead, at the top of a ridge, the bearded man waited, and with him waited safety. Grinding his teeth against pain and weariness, Kurt climbed on.

CHAPTER 9

Deep in the forest, Tostri raced along in the wake of his quarry. Edon had run away from camp at full speed, and as far as Tostri could tell, he had not slowed.

Two things helped Tostri follow the trail. One was Edon's scent, made much stronger by the bark armor that he wore. Its distinctive aroma lingered even in the air, and at places where Edon had brushed against leaves, the air was thick with it. The second aid was the visual record Edon had left. In small clearings, where the thin drizzle wet the ground, his three-toed footprints showed plain. Even in the depths of the forest, Edon had taken no particular care to mask his trail. Tostri would see a broken twig here, a crushed leaf there. He realized that Edon, with no great opinion of Tostri's chances, might even be making things easy for him.

But that was because Edon was sure he could win the stalking game. Tostri remembered the contempt that Eklok had expressed when he had learned that

Tostri could not hear. Edon would feel something of the same emotion. Or would he feel pity?

Either way, Tostri did not care. For him the important goal was to find the young hunter, then to take the red token from him. Nothing else mattered. And if Edon thought his tracker could not possibly keep up with him, so much the better. Perhaps the young hunter would grow careless or make a mistake.

Sunset was still many hours away. Tostri wondered how far his quarry would go and when he would circle back. So far, the trail led away from the hunters' camp.

Tostri slowed as he approached a small clearing. Trails led from it in two directions—or three, if he counted the one he was on. Which way had Edon gone? Pausing at the edge of the clearing, Tostri looked carefully at the ground. Dinosaur vision was not quite like human vision. Humans saw what they called "visible light," but dinosaurs could see farther into the spectrum than humans. Infrared light gave them a whole world of colors that humans could not see.

And in that light, Edon's footprints lingered, not pressed into the ground, but shining a shadowy brownish red on the surface. The glow was very faint. In full sun, it might not be visible at all. The overcast, drizzly sky helped. Tostri considered. The trail seemed to lead to his left. But Edon was a hunter. He was also a Deinonychus, with a full awareness of dinosaur vision. Would he leave such an obvious trail? That seemed unlikely.

After a few seconds of thought, Tostri had an idea. He touched the tip of his tail to a sequoia. Then he stood on tiptoes and concentrated on the vibrations he felt. Some came through his extended toes. Others traveled through the deep roots of the tall tree and into the tip of his tail. Experimentally, Tostri moved around the trunk, pausing to analyze the vibrations he was picking up.

They told him that Edon was still running. Though hard to detect, the thumps of his footfalls came through in a muted rhythm. And because sound travels in waves, Tostri could sense a very small difference in timing. When he was in one position, the vibrations from the tree reached him the barest fraction of a second before those he felt with his toes. That told him that Edon was somewhere in a direct line beyond the tree. And that clue told Tostri that Edon had not taken the left path, after all. The vibrations tracked him off to the right. Tostri guessed that Edon must have left a deliberately misleading track leading down the left path. Ignoring the decoy footprints, Tostri hurried down the right trail in pursuit.

Not a hundred strides from the clearing, Tostri saw two pads of leaves tossed aside in the underbrush. Tangled with them were small vines. The pads would just fit a deinonychid foot. Tostri grunted soundlessly to himself in satisfaction. That explained the mystery of the footprints. Edon had gone a short way up the left path, then had fashioned the foot pads and had tied them to his feet. With the leaves obscuring the heat print of his feet, he had retraced his steps and had taken the right trail, throwing the pads away when he thought they had done their job. Now his footprints showed up again, glowing a little more brightly. Thanks to his trick—and to the fact that it had not fooled Tostri—Tostri had gained a little ground.

He sniffed carefully and smelled the lingering aroma of the cork-bark armor that Edon wore. It was faint, far fainter than he expected. Another trick? Perhaps the bark had a strong smell when fresh, and the scent rapidly faded. If so, that would add to Tostri's difficulties. He had to assume that was the case, then. It would not do to underestimate his prey. He could pick up Edon's scent, too, stronger now that the bark's aroma was not masking it. He would rely on that. For a moment, Tostri was tempted to race down the trail at top speed, closing in on Edon as fast as he could.

But he realized that if he simply ran, Edon would be alerted. Either he, too, would feel the vibrations of pursuit or he would hear the sounds that Tostri would make. Tostri decided that he was going to have to take a chance. The trail seemed to curve off to the right. Was the curve continuous? If so, then it looped back toward the deinonychids' camp. That seemed reasonable. Eklok would not expect a long hunt.

So Tostri could cut across the loop and join the

trail somewhere ahead of Edon. It was his best hope of not alerting his prey. Tostri plunged into the rainforest. The slope of the ground here made the trees grow a little farther apart, and the undergrowth was sometimes thick. Several times Tostri had to detour. Twice he paused to sense vibrations, and both times he could barely feel Edon somewhere far off. Now Edon was no longer running, but walking with long strides. Tostri was happy with that. Edon's confidence was giving him a chance to get ahead.

He splashed across a sluggish stream, climbed a low rise, and then skirted an enormous tangle of deadfall trees left by some storm. Insects zipped past, and from the forest canopy a steady drip of rain pattered on him. Tostri could run all day in open country, but making his way through the forest began to tire him. He could never keep a straight path, and sometimes the footing was tricky, being either slippery mud or piles of leaves.

Then when he was wondering if he had chosen the right course, he burst through a thicket of ferns and saw a trail ahead of him. Was it the right one? Carefully slowing his breathing, he stood on the tips of his toes and waited.

No vibrations.

Tostri clenched his teeth. That could mean he was on the wrong track entirely. Edon might have taken another path. Or perhaps he was far ahead of Edon, so far that he could no longer feel his footfalls. Or Edon

74

might be walking slowly and carefully now, so his footsteps did not announce themselves so clearly.

So many possibilities. Tostri sniffed the path, the ferns alongside it, the lower tree branches. He could find no trace of the armor's scent. At least Edon had not passed this way.

Tostri followed the trail. When it dipped into a low, marshy place, he saw some footprints in the mud. They were far from fresh, probably days old. But they were deinonychid prints. The hunters seemed very territorial. It was a fair assumption that the prints had been left by Eklok's hunters. So they did use this path.

Tostri considered his options. He realized that he could not simply stand and wait to see if Edon was coming. His trek through the forest had showed him that Edon could easily get away from him merely by dashing off the trail and into the undergrowth. Edon knew the countryside. Tostri did not.

So how to surprise his prey, assuming he was in the right place? Edon was a hunter and probably in top physical condition. He might be faster than Tostri in a race. Tostri had to find some way of hiding so he could surprise Edon.

Tostri had been slowly making his way up the trail as he thought. He came to another dip in the trail, where a small stream cut across. It had eroded the soil down to volcanic bedrock. Standing on the rock and concentrating hard, Tostri felt the regular trace of Edon's footfalls. He waited long enough to make sure they were slowly growing stronger. Edon was walking now. Very likely he was confident that he had thrown Tostri off his trail.

Now if only Tostri could find some place to hide. He stood at the edge of the stream and studied his surroundings. A banyan tree grew right at the edge of the forest. A member of the fig family, it had dozens of crooked, writhing branches sprouting from its trunk, starting just a couple of feet off the ground.

A thought occurred to Tostri. Kurt climbed trees. Dinosaurs didn't—well, not deinonychids, anyway!

If he could manage to scramble up into the banyan, he could perch just above the trail. It would be the last place Edon would expect Tostri to be. The thick leaves would provide good cover. And the height would let him have a good view of Edon's approach.

Tostri took a cautious step onto the lowest branch. It felt unsteady, though he clenched his toes tightly. Steadying himself with his hands, he pulled up to the next branch, and then the next. They dipped and bent with his weight, and he paused twice, feeling dizzy. This was different from flying. Somehow the danger of falling seemed more real and more immediate when he depended on these springy branches for support!

Tostri forced himself upward, though climbing was far from easy. He slipped three or four times, and once he barely kept himself from plummeting to the ground. The branches swayed alarmingly, but they held under his weight.

But at last, Tostri lay stretched out along a strong branch. Leaves surrounded him, though he had selected a spot where he had a view of the trail through a break in the foliage. He was not terribly far from the ground, perhaps twice his own height. Still, looking down made him feel queasy. The drizzling rain cooled him, and a light breeze made the branch dip and sway in a gentle motion.

He stared down at the trail. Thirty strides away from his tree, it curved sharply off to the left. Edon would appear there, if he had judged correctly. The wind was coming from that direction, so Edon would not be able to smell him. But Tostri might be able to catch Edon's scent before the hunter actually came into view.

For what seemed like a long time, but probably was just a few minutes, Tostri kept his senses alert. Then he did smell something, the scent of the bark armor. It was a lot fainter than it had been, but the odor was unmistakable. A moment later, Edon came into view. No longer running, the hunter strode along. Edon's whole attitude showed that he was straining every sense himself. His expression was alert, wary. Just at the bend in the trail, Edon paused, shifting his weight from foot to foot and looking back the way he had come. To Tostri, Edon looked uneasy. He twitched his tail and bent his head as if listening.

Then he turned and looked down the trail, in Tostri's direction. Edon's head jerked in short arcs as his sharp eyes searched the landscape. Tostri froze, clinging to the banyan branch, hoping that the leaves concealed him. At last Edon came toward him, with cautious, slow steps.

He must have a hunter's instincts, Tostri thought. *There's no way he could know I'm close, but something tells him to be careful.*

Tostri held his breath. Edon came to the edge of the shallow stream and bent to drink. After a few seconds, his nostrils quivered. He straightened suddenly, staring hard down the trail. He grunted, a quiet, questioning sound.

He's caught my scent, Tostri thought, willing Edon to take just two more strides.

The young hunter took one step. He stood in the middle of the stream, sniffing the air suspiciously. Then, slowly, he took a second step. . . .

And Tostri pounced!

To be honest, he fell more than pounced. He rolled free of the branch and fell feetfirst. His claws clenched the armor on Edon's back, and he snapped his teeth at the scarf.

Just as Tostri grabbed the armor, Edon sprang ahead, but he was too late. Tostri was on his back, and the hunter stumbled, fell sprawling in the ferns at the edge of the trail. He tried to roll, to throw Tostri off. Tostri clung hard, jerking at the red scarf.

Then Edon made a huge effort and lurched to his feet. Twisting, he slammed Tostri into the trunk of the banyan hard enough to jar him loose. Tostri landed on his feet just as Edon took off at a run, trying to cross the stream and backtrack. With a leap, Tostri snatched at the scarf again. Trying to dodge, Edon lost his footing in the slippery streambed and splashed down with Tostri right over him.

Still, Edon was not ready to surrender. He scrambled up to his feet again and warily circled, looking for an opening. *Prey can be dangerous,* Eklok had warned. Tostri didn't think that Edon would really try to hurt him, but his opponent was not ready to give up the token without a struggle. Edon was seeking a way of escape.

His move almost caught Tostri off guard. With a sudden half-turn, Edon thrashed out with his tail, trying to trip Tostri. Tostri leaped almost straight up, avoiding the blow. He leaped again, anticipating Edon's return thrash, and at the height of his second leap, he stretched his neck out and closed his teeth on the scarf again.

His weight made Edon stumble and fall, and as he fell, Tostri pulled the scarf free. For a moment, the two deinonychids did not move. Tostri stood with the scarf dangling from his teeth. He was breathing hard.

Edon crouched before him, eyes wide with surprise. Then, slowly, Edon rose. He said something that Tostri could not interpret. Tostri blinked very slowly, a deinonychid way of silently asking a question: *What do you mean?*

Seeming to understand, Edon jerked his head

downward three times. Then he extended his neck, chin pointing upward.

Tostri got the idea: prey that falls three times is helpless. The contest was over, and Edon would not question Tostri's ownership of the red scarf.

Tostri had won.

But what about Kurt? And what about the unknown danger?

Tostri gestured: *We must get back to camp quickly.*

Edon responded with a simple, easily understood motion: *Follow me.*

The two deinonychids raced down the trail, no longer opponents. Now they were fighting together against time and the unknown.

CHAPTER 10

Using the spear as a walking stick, Kurt had been climbing steadily, trying to keep to the edge of the stream. At places the rocky hillside was too steep for that. Then he had to leave the stream and travel through the fringes of the rainforest. Always, though, the thunder of the cascades was a guide. It kept him going when he hit tangles of fallen tree branches, jumbled piles of smooth gray boulders, places where he had to creep along on his two feet and his one good hand.

Thinking was still hard, but he had a blind, dogged determination to follow the stream, to find the ridge, to rejoin his . . . father.

That was the word. *Father.*

The gray rain still swept down in gauzy curtains. It did not let up, but it grew no harder. Kurt felt as if he had never been dry. The cool rain should have helped the pain in his hand, but that thudded sharply with every heartbeat. His head felt worse, too. When he grew dizzy and the violet haze began to appear, Kurt rested, but the pain in his hand always forced him up again. He had to get to the bearded man. He had to find help.

One step. Then another.

For some time, he had been climbing toward a formidable barrier. At a place where the cascades shot down at a steep angle, boiling into white water and spray, its banks became two high dark gray cliffs, pitted and weathered, splotched with pale green lichens and darker green moss. The cliff on his side was unclimbable. It reared almost vertically thirty or forty feet. Kurt hesitated, looking doubtfully into the forest. Under the overcast sky, its shadows had grown deep and dark. A confused image of the crocodile-headed creature came to him, a sense of great danger.

But there was no other way. He could not cross the stream; he could not climb the cliff; he lacked the strength to double back.

Taking a deep breath, Kurt skirted the foot of the cliff. The rock underfoot had gained a thick covering of spongy moss over the centuries. It was springy underfoot—and treacherous. One misstep could send Kurt tumbling. He carefully squelched along until the ground leveled a hundred yards or more from the cascades. Now he was in the forest. Breathing rapidly, Kurt scurried along, his spear held at the ready.

The thick canopy overhead shielded him from most of the rain. The still, humid air zinged and chirred with insects and amphibians. Kurt's soaked clothes stuck to him in a clammy embrace, chafed his arms and legs as he walked.

His path lay uphill, though the slope in the forest was not nearly as steep as along the riverbank. Kurt was clambering over a fallen, vine-swathed tree trunk when a distant sound made him freeze.

A harsh, deep bellow of challenge rang out from somewhere far ahead. Its echoes quickly died. Kurt could not keep from flattening himself against the tree trunk, trying to hide. For a minute or more, he pressed himself down, his heart hammering inside his chest.

At last a noisy insect that had been startled to silence by the roar began to make its cry again, a sound like something frying. Other insects joined in. Something nearby began to croak a plaintive *whonnk!* Kurt closed his eyes. He knew the sound. In his mind, he visualized the source. It was a blue-green frog as large as his hand, with a voice that belonged to a much bigger animal.

Harmless, though. That creature, called a Triadobatrachus he remembered, was dangerous only to small insects. Kurt slipped over the trunk and began to work his way back to the left. The thunder of the cascades grew steadily louder in his ears, and at last he was in sight of them again.

He had bypassed the cliff. Here he could approach the edge of the stream. Now he stood perhaps half a mile from the head of the cascades, but the climb was relatively gentle. Kurt left the shadow of the forest and walked on the margin of the stream, compacted black sand. Sometimes the bank grew steeper and he had to wade. Behind him the cascades roiled down and down over stones, sending spumes of spray high into the air. It was a wonder he had survived that plunge with nothing more to show than a few scrapes and bruises.

Step after step, and the stream began to behave itself, lost its white-water ferocity. Now it was a broad river again, its currents swift but not deadly. Kurt walked on in the drizzle, his legs numb. The dreary rain continued, crawling down his face.

Soon he neared the spot where the river split and ran around either side of a green teardrop-shaped island. The upper end had collected piles of gray, smooth driftwood. Reeds grew thick and green along the whole island's length, but here and there round gray boulders projected above the swaying tips of the reeds.

Kurt rubbed his eyes. He thought his vision was playing tricks again. Then he realized that the day was growing dark. The sun had sunk low, and soon it would set. Could he continue walking? He was staggering with exhaustion already. And—

The earth shook.

Kurt stumbled and fell to his knees, throwing out his hands to break his fall. He could not keep from gasping when his injured palm slammed into the sand.

Pain like hot white light shot up his arm.

Kurt scrambled into the water, spinning, staring at the rainforest for any sign of the crocodile-headed creature. His first confused thought had been that it was charging him, that its heavy footfalls were shaking the foundations of the earth. But the creature did not appear.

A second tremor hit. Kurt saw the water itself splash and leap. Then he remembered an image, a mountain crowned with a plume of steam and smoke. An . . . what was the word? An earthquake. That was the cause of the shock. He could not see the volcano from here, but somewhere far in the distance, it was rumbling and heaving.

The second tremor seemed to go on for far too long. At last Kurt realized that his legs were shaking. He was so tired he was on the edge of collapse. And the world was edged in violet again. He had to rest.

Twenty feet away from him was the green island. He realized it might be a place of refuge. Perhaps nothing could find him there.

He waded deeper. The water came to his waist, the current tugging him toward the cascades. Kurt leaned against it, slipped and stumbled, losing ground. Still he fought his way on, and the water became shallower. With a gasp, Kurt crawled up onto the island's shore at last, like an exhausted dolphinback, one of those shipwrecked humans brought to shore by Dinotopia's

85

friendly, intelligent dolphins. He had to push his way through the thick reeds, trying to find some sort of shelter.

The island rose like the back of a turtle. Near the top of the rise, Kurt found a tiny clearing, no more than six feet across. Its floor was the gray surface of a boulder, nearly flat. Not far away lay dozens of tree branches, driftwood left by some flood.

Instinct kicked in again, or perhaps training did. Kurt dragged the branches over, propped them against each other, interwove the twigs. Soon he had made a rough framework, low but sufficient. Then he went to work breaking reeds off, bringing them back in armloads. Weaving their springy stalks in and out of the driftwood frame, Kurt built up a temporary shelter, a low green dome thatched with reeds. More reeds piled inside made a makeshift mattress.

As the last light faded, Kurt crept inside the hut. Everything was damp, but the shelter was snug enough. No rain dripped through.

Lying on his stomach, Kurt stared out as the last light of day faded. All around him, he could hear the flow of the river. From downstream, faint now, came the grumble of the cascades. He closed his eyes for a moment and opened them in complete darkness. Kurt realized he had fallen asleep. Rain had wakened him, a heavier rain that pattered on the reeds above his head. Wind stirred the standing reeds on the island, gusts that mingled with faraway thunder.

No water dripped through onto him, though. He had built his shelter well. He couldn't say that he was dry—his soaked clothing still clung to his back, arms, and legs—but at least he wasn't getting any wetter.

A flicker of lightning showed him the windblown reeds, and beyond them a dark stretch of the river. For a time, he waited to hear the thunder, but when it came, it was faint. He sighed and closed his eyes again.

Kurt fell asleep once more. And he dreamed . . .

The deinonychids. They surrounded the island, waving their spears in the air, sending shrill, threatening cries his way. Threats? Or . . . warnings, perhaps? Warnings about what? In the dream, the dinosaurs seemed less frightening. Their outlandish attire— leather headbands sporting red, green, and yellow feathers, round shields, gray leather cloaks—seemed not as strange. Kurt had the feeling that they were trying to speak with him, trying to communicate some warning.

But what? The dream shifted, and now he saw the deinonychid hunters chasing down a wading bird, casting their spears. Kurt had never seen an animal killed. In his dream, the bird died in a shriek and an explosion of blood and feathers.

And then he was among a flock of the birds, huge ones, his size. They were clattering and squawking as they ran somewhere with desperate strides, their soft bodies bumping into him, jostling him. He tried to run, too, but he was too slow.

Then a shadow loomed over him, blotting out the sun. The dream became a nightmare. Kurt turned, looking up and up. The crocodile-headed dinosaur towered over him.

Suchomimus.

Kurt could not move.

The creature's head was as large as his whole body. The long snout gaped in a shark-toothed grin. The merciless brown eyes held him in their predatory glare.

Suchomimus, the crocodile mimic. Small numbers of them lived in the Rainy Basin, larger groups on a few of the outlying islands around Dinotopia. They were antisocial, grim loners. They ate fish.

Or anything they could catch with their enormous, wickedly curved foreclaws.

The creature stooped, opening its jaws. Kurt felt its hot breath on him, smelling strongly of decaying fish. The beast roared, shaking the world. Its jaws began to close over him—

With a shout, Kurt tried to spring to his feet. He bumped his head, and for a dizzying moment he was sure the monstrous dinosaur had him in its mouth.

Then he felt the rustling spring of reeds. No. He had been dreaming. He was in his hut on the island, safe—

A challenging scream split the night.

The creature was somewhere close.

And it sounded hungry.

CHAPTER 11

Tostri and Edon had returned to the deinonychid hunters' camp at sunset, too late to go looking for Kurt. Now the hunters gathered around a low campfire, its red light casting deep shadows as they sat in a circle, paying close attention to their leader. Tostri stood before him, feeling conspicuous. Eklok had ceremonially tied the red scarf around his neck. Tostri wore it with a strange mixture of pride and embarrassment. True, it was a mark of achievement. However, Tostri knew that part of his victory had been luck, and despite the excitement of the chase, he was no hunter.

To Tostri's right, Stanhope Ramos stood at the edge of the circle, impatiently. Tostri knew what he was feeling. He felt it himself: concern for Kurt, an eagerness to begin the hunt. But he realized that what Eklok was telling him meant that they could not begin until daybreak.

Tostri gestured for a pause in Eklok's story. He turned to the healer and explained: *Eklok says that Kurt is across the river. The territory belongs to*—Tostri carefully spelled out the name that Eklok had given him—*Jagga*.

"What is Jagga?" demanded Stanhope, his forehead wrinkled with worry.

Tostri noticed that Eklok's hunters stirred uneasily when Stanhope pronounced the name. He suspected that they had some sort of superstition about speaking it aloud. None of them objected, though. Tostri explained: *That is their name for a large carnivorous dinosaur. I believe Jagga is a Suchomimus.*

"Here?" Stanhope asked, his expression one of surprise. "I thought the only ones of that kind lived in the Rainy Basin."

Tostri's hands wove his answer in the air: *On Dinotopia, yes, that is right. But the Suchomimus group are fish-eaters. In the dim past, many of them swam to the small islands off the coast of Dinotopia. They are very territorial. This one came to Outer Island from a place Eklok calls "Fish Island." Jagga has been here for many years. He is a loner, a rogue, perhaps even an outcast from his own tribe.*

Stanhope looked around at the deinonychids. "They seem to fear this Jagga," he said. "Is he truly a danger?"

Tostri tried to communicate what he had learned from Eklok. *There is a truce between Jagga and the other dinosaurs on Outer Island. Jagga has his fishing grounds, all along the other side of the river as far as the base of Brightfire Mountain and down to something* called the Rushing Falls. If Eklok's people do not stray into his territory, he does not bother them. But Jagga regards everything on his side of the river as prey.

"We'll have to reason with Jagga," Stanhope said. "Surely, he'll understand that Kurt is no threat to his territory. Maybe we can give him a tribute of fish for passage."

Tostri relayed this possibility to Eklok, who replied at some length. Then Tostri turned back to Stanhope. *Eklok says Jagga does not negotiate. He believes life is hunting, slaying, and devouring. Eklok believes Jagga's way of life is too savage even for Jagga's own kind. That could be why he came to Outer Island.*

With frustration and anxiety struggling on his face, Stanhope asked Eklok, "Will Jagga attack my son? Would he attack a helpless boy?"

Eklok lowered his head. Tostri knew that it was all too possible that the rogue Suchomimus would attack Kurt. Such creatures were not picky eaters. Like most of the big meat-eaters, they loved fish, but they would eat anything they could catch. If Jagga was indeed as territorial as Eklok had indicated, then he would regard any intruder as a challenge, even one so obviously harmless as Kurt.

Stanhope sighed and asked Eklok to tell them what the deinonychids knew of Kurt.

Yes, the hunters had seen a boy whose description matched Kurt's appearance, Eklok signed. They'd tried to warn him about the danger he was in—for the boy was on Jagga's side of the river. He did not seem to understand either their speech or their gestures, though, and ran away. Worse, the deinonychids had twice heard Jagga's warning cries that day, cries that told other predators to stay away from his territory. Jagga was across the river, and not far off.

Tostri asked, *Will Jagga take a tribute of fish? Where we live, the large meat-eaters love fish and will permit travel through their lands in exchange for them.*

Eklok's toss of the head conveyed amusement. "Who doesn't like fish?" he asked, and Tostri could lip-read that simple phrase. Then, with gestures, he elaborated: *Perhaps. Hard to say. Jagga never has enough food. We will try. While you and the human rest, some of my hunters will use their fishing nets. What fish we take, we will offer to Jagga.*

But despite Eklok's advice, neither Tostri nor Stanhope could rest. They went with the fishing party to the broad pool. The deinonychids set up a flaring torch on a bamboo pole stuck deep into the black sand. Its orange flame leaped and flickered. Tostri knew that it would not burn for very long. The rain had become harder, steadier, and flickers of lightning occasionally lit the sky. Before much fishing could be done, the rain would put out the torch.

But the hunters knew exactly what they were doing. They waited for a while, and Tostri could see quick, silvery shapes flashing just below the surface of the pool. The light on shore attracted the interest of the abundant fish. They shoaled together, gliding back and forth, fascinated by the strange red glare.

When the water was thick with them, two of the hunters waded out into the pool. They carried with them a long net, woven from thin, flexible vines. Slowly, they spread the net wide, until they had isolated the edge of the pool closest to the torch. Then they rushed forward, dragging the net in a narrowing arc.

Tostri saw it sweep through the water. He could see the frantic flash of leaping fish, the occasional silvery dart as one got away. Many more blundered into the net, though, and when the hunters dragged it ashore, they had a good catch of fish, enough to provide a feast for Eklok and all his hunters.

But would it be enough of a tribute? When he was much younger, Tostri had seen one Suchomimus. He recalled a thirty-five-foot-long predator, its head long and snouted, out of proportion to the rest of its body. Such a creature needed enormous amounts of food, and like all the bigger meat-eaters, it seemed to be always hungry. Provisions that would feed Eklok's hunters for a week would provide one hearty meal for such a predator.

The night grew darker, the rain heavier, and they all retreated to camp. There beneath the forest canopy, everything was comparatively dry. The two fishermen began to hang their catch on a lean-to frame near the fire, smoking them. That would keep them from decaying and would add to their taste.

Finally, well after midnight, Eklok insisted that Stanhope and Tostri go to bed for the night. He offered one of the hunters' huts, and Tostri found it a snug haven. Stanhope prepared a mat of dried grasses and lay on it. For a long time, he remained there, stretched out on his back, his arms crossed and his hands behind his head. Tostri crouched nearby, his infrared vision showing him Stanhope's restless tossing and turning. At last in the darkness, the healer said, "Tostri? If you're awake, touch my hand."

Tostri reached out and touched Stanhope's outstretched hand.

"I wanted to thank you," Stanhope said in the darkness. "You did not have to take that challenge. We could have risked going after Kurt ourselves. But it's better that you did gain Eklok's respect. If Kurt is anywhere around, I think Eklok's hunters can surely find him. And you did well, my friend. I think that from now on, Eklok's hunters will not be so quick to assume that someone who is different can't do all the things they can do. That is always a lesson worth learning, and one my people sometimes forget. Thank you, my friend."

Tostri could not reply by gesture, for it was too dark for Stanhope to see. But he grasped Stanhope's hand.

Sometime after that, with the smell of rain and distant lightning in his nostrils, Tostri fell asleep.

* * *

Morning woke him: the milky light of an overcast day, though the rain had stopped. Stanhope lay asleep. Tostri carefully arose and left the hut. In the central clearing of the hunters' camp, a lone guard stood leaning on his spear. He nodded at Tostri in a friendly way. Then he lifted his head and gave out a call that Tostri could not hear.

The entire camp came to life at once. Eklok came from his hut, sniffing the air. He gestured to Tostri: *A good morning to hunt. When you are ready, we begin.*

Stanhope emerged from the hut he had shared with Tostri. "When can we start?" he asked.

At once, Eklok says, Tostri replied. *Will you eat first?*

With an impatient shake of his head, Stanhope said, "I'm not hungry. Let's go."

Eklok, Edon, and one other hunter, an older male named Ezkar, would be the hunting party. Tostri and Edon carried the fish, a heavy weight even after a night of drying before a smoky fire. Ezkar, whose headgear wore a fan of bright feathers and whose features were scarred, took the lead. *He is our oldest hunter,* Eklok explained to Tostri. *No one can follow a track like Ezkar. He is not as strong as a young hunter, but his senses are sharp.*

They reached the edge of the pool, waded in, and emerged on the far side. For a long time, they followed the course of the stream, wading in the shallows when the banks grew too steep. Then one of the hunters signed for a halt.

Eklok had the rest of them stand at the edge of the water while Ezkar went back and forth along the rocky shore, bending close to the ground, his eyes intent and his nostrils twitching. Then he straightened and said something to Eklok.

"What is it?" Stanhope asked. "I couldn't follow that."

Eklok explained it through sign language: *The hunters followed Kurt this far. Now Ezkar has the trace. The boy fled downstream. We can follow his trail. But be alert. Ezkar says Jagga is nearby.*

They set off downstream. With the heavy fish carried in a basket on his back, Tostri leaned forward. He kept his eyes on the rainforest. It glistened with last night's shower, and tendrils of ground mist flowed out of it, curling down to the stream. Its dim depths could hide anything.

Was Jagga there, watching them? If the Suchomimus caught them on his territory, would they be able to negotiate? Would they even have time?

Impossible to say, Tostri decided. For now, his task was not to lead, but to follow. Ezkar could find Kurt, if anyone could. Tostri only hoped that Ezkar could sense Jagga, too. At least in time to give them some sort of warning.

As the sun rose, the search party hurried along, heading down the river. Tostri had to admire the old hunter's skill. Once in a great while, Tostri could see some sign of Kurt's passing: a blurred footprint in the sand, a faint trail of bent reeds. But Ezkar never seemed to have any doubt or to lose touch with the clues that Tostri could barely notice.

The sun rose invisibly behind the white overcast. They came to a bend of the stream, and Ezkar suddenly signaled a halt. He and Eklok had a hurried conversation.

Looking past them, Tostri saw the reason. Another footprint in a low, muddy spot.

But this one was not Kurt's.

Tostri swallowed hard as he looked at the enormous three-toed imprint.

Jagga.

He had to be close by. The footprint was still filling with water, a slow ooze. And judging from the size of the print, Jagga had to be truly enormous.

But Tostri had little time to worry about that. Eklok signaled again, and they all hurried on. A chilling thought struck Tostri: Jagga was a hunter, too.

What if, like Ezkar, Jagga were following Kurt's trail?

How far ahead was the fearsome predator?

And how far ahead was Kurt?

CHAPTER 12

For hours Kurt had crouched in his makeshift hut, wakeful and worried. Gray light spread in the world outside, a cloudy dawn, but without rain. Kurt felt dizzy, as if the island beneath him were rocking back and forth. He knew he should be hungry, but his stomach crawled with nausea. His hand wasn't as sore as it had been, but the swollen fingers felt stiff, and the spines he had not been able to dig out burned in the flesh of his palm. Worse, the swelling was creeping up his forearm. If he did not find help soon . . .

He carefully crept out of his hiding place and stood knee-deep in curling ground mist. The river was invisible beneath it. Kurt listened. He had heard nothing more since that one earth-shaking roar hours before dawn. Had the beast passed by? Had it been following his scent, but lost it at the point where Kurt had plunged into the river?

There was no way of knowing. Feeling hot and shaky, Kurt focused his mind on the bearded man, the healer. He had to find the healer. His way lay . . . upstream. Kurt studied his options. He could see that the left side of the river was still a bluff bank, with mist cascading over the top and curling down to the surface. The right bank was still his only hope. It was level enough for him to wade along the edge of the streambed.

He groaned as he stepped into the water. His muscles ached from exertion, and the bumps and bruises he had received while tumbling down the cascades made themselves known with every step. Kurt dragged himself against the current until he stood ankle-deep at the edge of the river, his clothes feeling heavier than ever. Shivering, he began to plod upstream, the ground fog so thick that he could not see his feet.

How long he kept this up, he could not say. In his daze, he knew that he was not traveling fast. He had shot down the cascades in a matter of minutes, but staggering and stumbling back upstream was another matter.

Kurt drifted to the edge of consciousness and back. Aching in every joint, sick and disoriented, he knew only that he had to keep going. At some point, he stumbled on a round stone, fell forward, and caught himself with his hands, grinding his teeth to keep from yelling out at the pain from his injured palm.

Groggy, he pushed himself up and became aware that he could see the ground again. A watery sun had broken through the clouds. It was late morning, with the sun high already. In his damp clothes, Kurt still shivered. He knew it was not really cold, but he felt as if he would never be warm again.

He remembered a time when he had fallen into a cold pool. Someone—a dinosaur—had helped him out then. Someone had led him to a warming fire. His friend. Who was his friend? Images flashed in his mind: a library in Waterfall City, a fireplace sending out welcome heat. A dry hillside with—Tostri? Yes, that was his friend's name, Tostri—beside him, the sun hot on their skins as they watched Skybaxes gliding high overhead.

And another glimpse of the bearded man, of fa—fa—

"Father," Kurt said, his voice a hoarse croak. "Father. S-Stanhope Ramos. M-my father." He knew that Stanhope was at a camp, high on a ridge.

If he had strength enough to reach it. Kurt forced himself to get up and move. He felt his collection pouch, thrust inside his shirt. His injured hand rested on it.

The land was rising again, the river to his left narrowing and rushing over hidden rocks. A flock of brown and gray Archaeopteryx splashed at the edge of the stream. At his approach, they yipped and took to the air with a noisy clatter of wings.

At last Kurt had to pause and rest. He drank a little from the river. Immediately, he threw it up again. He sat on a fallen log in a thicket of ferns. The sun had faded behind clouds again, and the lightest drizzle had started to fall. Rainforest. That's why they called this the rainforest. Kurt wondered how far he had to go. He had been creeping along, making perhaps half a mile in an hour—or had he been traveling for that long? Two minutes of struggling through the water's edge seemed like an hour.

Sitting with his eyes closed, Kurt heard a screech from somewhere not far away, then another. He opened his eyes and stood up. The sounds came from downstream, and a moment later, he saw a pink explosion as a cloud of Pterodaustros burst into the air above the forest edge. The creatures were wading pterosaurs, five feet long, their skin a mottled pink and gray. Their deep, gooselike squawks showed that something had alarmed them.

The pterosaurs fled in a ragged V formation, their wings beating. They passed overhead, gabbling and honking. Kurt swallowed. Whatever had spooked them was not so very far away. He hurried on, wading through the edge of the river. But before he had gone a hundred steps, he heard something else. It was a deep, gruff growl, then the rustle of something big moving fast.

Kurt looked wildly around. The river was no refuge, not here. The current in midstream would sweep his feet from under him if he tried to wade, and weak as he was, Kurt doubted that he could survive.

In the other direction, up the steep streambank, was the forest.

Loops of lianas hung from some of the trees, and one looked low enough for him to reach. Kurt dropped his spear and ran to it. He gave it an experimental tug with his good left hand. It would hold his weight.

Kurt closed both hands on the vine. He grimaced, and sweat broke out on his forehead as he pulled himself free of the ground. His injured right hand pulsed with pain.

But he had no choice. Kurt hauled himself up, inch by inch. Fifteen feet from the ground, the vine draped over a tree branch. He hauled himself onto it, then clambered for the next branch, higher over his head. His muscles strained, and he gasped for breath. Kicking, scrambling, somehow he pulled himself higher and higher, until he could go no farther. He had reached a spot where he could sit straddling one branch, with a smaller one under his left arm and his back pressed against the tree trunk. Black spots swirled and swam in front of his eyes, and blood pounded in his ears.

How high was he? Forty, fifty feet. Far off the ground. He couldn't afford to faint. Kurt clutched the branches tightly. Was he safe?

More shrieks of startled birds or pterosaurs, from very nearby. Movement on the ground beneath. Kurt strained to see what it was. Something humped and low to the ground came blundering toward the tree. A glyptodont, and a young one, Kurt realized. It was three feet long, with a rounded, hard, turtle-like shell and a tail that ended in a macelike spiked ball. Something had alarmed it, and it hurried as well as it could, hissing. It plunged into a thicket of ferns and vanished from sight.

Then something else heaved into view. It was huge.

A striped, light and dark green body, with two heavy forearms bearing hooked, knifelike claws. A long-snouted head, the mouth open in a toothy grin.

Kurt held on to the branch even harder, tried to flatten himself into invisibility. This was the creature that had roared in the night. The one that had haunted his nightmares.

Suchomimus, the crocodile mimic. The creature walked with a purposeful gait, its long body almost horizontal to the earth, its dangling front claws clenching and unclenching. It must have come from downstream, passing him on the island as he slept. Then it had gone deep into the forest, but something, his scent, perhaps, had called it back toward the river. It sniffed, its nostrils flaring. Deep brown eyes, flecked with yellow, darted this way and that. The enormous dinosaur stooped and snorted. Kurt saw that it was nosing the spear he had dropped.

It was on his trail!

The predator rumbled, an angry, deep sound.

Slowly, it rose, its eyes blinking. Swaying from side to side on its hind legs, the Suchomimus seemed to listen.

Kurt was afraid the predatory saurian could hear his heart. It pounded in his chest, giving him the energy that prey needed, energy to flee.

But he was no bird or pterosaur. He couldn't take to the air to escape. Nor was he an armored glyptodont, protected by a bony sheath of scutes. He was human, exposed and helpless before this creature whose body was longer than the gondola of the *Cloudclimber*. All he could do was hide, and hope that the Suchomimus did not look up.

The meat-eater circled slowly, coming closer to Kurt's tree. It was probably trying to sort out the scents it detected, Kurt realized. The liana he had climbed snagged the dinosaur's jaw. With an impatient flick of its head, the creature snapped the vine with a loud pop. Then it stood for a moment, growling. It straightened, sniffing again. When it reared up, its head was no more than ten feet below Kurt's level.

It stood like that for a moment, then looked toward the river. Dropping back down, the Suchomimus stalked to the stream edge. It took a step into the rushing water, paused with its head cocked to one side, and then snapped. Kurt saw a silver flash as the predator snapped a three-foot-long salmon from the river. The fish curved into the air.

Then, with another snap, the Suchomimus swallowed the salmon whole.

While its attention was elsewhere, Kurt slowly forced himself to stand on his tree branch. If the creature could leap, he was far from safe. He imagined those long, toothy jaws closing on his legs. He had to get higher.

Kurt stepped up onto the branch that had been under his arm. From there he could reach the next branch, and he dragged himself up. The Suchomimus snatched another fish from the river as Kurt tried for the next branch.

Then he slipped, and for a moment Kurt felt he was falling. He sat down hard on the branch he had been standing on, and his flailing left hand grabbed another hanging vine. He caught himself just in time.

But he had made noise. The Suchomimus straightened instantly, its huge head whipping around, its brown eyes glaring in his direction. Kurt froze.

But the eyes narrowed. The creature had seen him.

The predator charged at once, bellowing a challenge. It came to the foot of the tree and stared up at Kurt, now a good fifteen feet above its head. It roared again, and Kurt could feel and smell its breath, hot and reeking of fish.

Kurt's instincts told him to climb, climb as fast and as high as he could.

But his body could not obey. He was played out, exhausted. It was all he could do to cling to his branch. The carnivorous dinosaur backed off, its tail lashing as if in anger. It roared again and shook its head.

Kurt's conscious mind kept trying to override his fear. The words that he had begun to recapture kept trying to tell him something: dinosaurs and humans lived together. They did not have to be prey and predator.

And, opposed to that, his vision told him the monster beneath his dangling feet would eat him.

The Suchomimus tilted its head, glaring at Kurt. It snapped its jaws twice. Then, suddenly, it crouched and leaped. Its teeth clashed together on the branch just below Kurt, and the limb snapped like a twig.

The dinosaur landed with a thud that Kurt felt. It jerked its head and tossed the branch toward the river. A moment later, the branch crashed to the riverbank.

Kurt's lungs were pumping. From the fog of memory, more words drifted into his mind, words of greeting, of peaceful intent. He shouted them as loudly as he could, his hoarse voice straining: *"Breathe deep! Seek peace!"*

What language he spoke, dinosaurian or human, he could not have said. At the sound of his voice, the predator seemed to pause, staring at him. Just for an instant, Kurt thought he might have gotten through to it, might have made it understand that he was no enemy. And no prey, for both he and the dinosaur shared intelligence, awareness—

But then it snarled. With a lunge, it threw itself against the trunk of Kurt's tree. The tree was sturdy, soaring a hundred feet or more, and its roots must have been deep.

But the Suchomimus weighed five tons. It crashed into the tree.

The branch Kurt was on thrashed like a twig. Kurt clasped it desperately, but he knew he could not hold on forever.

The Suchomimus retreated a few steps, then charged again. Kurt heard the tree trunk groan as the dinosaur crashed into it. He hugged the branch even tighter, knowing it was hopeless.

He would fall the next time, or the time after that. Fall right into the clutches of the crocodile-headed predator.

Kurt didn't have breath enough left even to scream.

CHAPTER 13

By mid-morning Eklok's party had come to a temporary halt. Even Ezkar was having trouble following an old trail through water, and he and Eklok conferred as the other dinosaurs ate a quick meal. The healer shook his head at the offer of food. Like Stanhope Ramos, Tostri had little appetite, but even so, the aroma of the fish made his mouth water. He shifted the straps of his basket slightly, easing the burden. He knew that Stanhope wanted to move faster, but he also knew that Ezkar was proceeding with a hunter's care. To speed up might mean losing the trail.

Indeed, Ezkar stopped and hesitated as if unsure. He gestured to Eklok: *The boy left no trace here. I will go downstream a few strides. You wait.*

Tostri passed this along to Stanhope. "I wish we could call out for him," the healer said. "He may be within hearing distance."

Eklok said something to him, and Stanhope translated that for Tostri: "He says Jagga is very near. The hunters have seen him fishing this stretch of the river for three or four days. We can't risk calling for Kurt. We might bring Jagga down on us instead."

They stood in a small group while Ezkar cautiously explored along the river shore. Suddenly, they all stiffened—all except Tostri. He signed, *What happened? What is it?*

"A sound," Stanhope explained. "A roar. It came from downstream."

Ezkar hurried back from the edge of the river. He and Eklok carried on a brief conversation, and then Eklok jerked his chin: *Follow me.* He took the lead. Clearly, they were no longer trackers. Tostri guessed that Eklok had decided the party had to investigate the roar. He and Stanhope followed as they scrambled up the riverbank and headed for the fringes of the forest.

The deinonychids were ideal runners. They strode along, choosing the best way past boulders, clumps of fern, and stands of reeds. Tostri deliberately fell behind, keeping step with the slower Stanhope Ramos. Ahead, the others reached a deadfall, a clutter of fallen trees. Eklok leaped up onto it, choosing the way, like a child leaping up a flight of steps. Edon went next, and then the older, slower Ezkar. When Tostri and Stanhope got to the base of the barrier, Ezkar was just disappearing over the top.

Go first, Tostri signed, knowing how anxious Stanhope must be. The human had difficulty. He lacked the gripping talons of the deinonychids, and he was of slighter build. Still, he hauled himself up the barrier with determination, scrambling and clambering without a pause. Tostri was prepared to help, but his human companion needed no boosting. He made it to the top himself, climbed over, and an instant later, Tostri was over as well.

Eklok, Edon, and Ezkar were far ahead, vanishing into tall ferns at the edge of the forest. Tostri and Stanhope descended the deadfall, leaped off, and ran after them. They plunged into the ferny thicket, following the path broken by the three hunters. A moment later, they burst out; ahead of them, Tostri saw Ezkar. He raised a hand in a warning gesture: *Carefully!*

Two dozen strides later, they caught up with Eklok and Edon, who stood poised on their toes. Tostri sniffed. He could smell theropod, all right, a thick, stale odor of fish and blood. The big meat-eater had to be nearby, somewhere in the forest. Then Tostri straightened suddenly, excitement making his heart race. Another odor. He signed, *Kurt is near!* to Stanhope. Another sniff, and then he signed, *This way!*

He felt a vibration that came through the earth, a sharp, brief shock. Something large falling? It did not have quite that quality about it. A moment later, he felt a second one, and this time he was able to judge its direction. Tostri hurried into the forest, not noticing the others.

Tostri felt a third crash, closer. He dodged trees and leaped tangles of brush. Then, almost without warning, he burst into a clearing. Tostri skidded to a halt, staring in horror.

Fifty yards away, his friend Kurt sat perched in a tall tree, a tree dripping with swaying vines. At the base of the tree, reared high on its hind legs, was a Suchomimus, its vast head stretched upward. It snapped its jaws a few feet below Kurt's dangling feet, then snarled in frustration. The predator gave the tree a powerful shove. Tostri could see the vines sway from the impact, and he could tell that Kurt was having trouble hanging on.

Tostri felt Stanhope Ramos come up beside him. He put out a hand and kept the human from charging into the clearing. Turning to tell Eklok that now was the time to negotiate, Tostri blinked in surprise.

Eklok, Ezkar, and Edon were far down the trail. They stood in a loose group, staring wide-eyed at the clearing and at the huge Jagga. Tostri frantically signaled: *Come now! Help!*

Edon took a hesitant step forward, then paused. With a shock, Tostri realized that the three hunters had not been fully prepared to face down a raging Suchomimus. They had been fine guides, but now their nerve had failed them. Tostri remembered that Eklok's hunters had had run-ins with Jagga before. More than anyone, they knew the power and the danger of the big theropod.

Tostri looked at Stanhope, touched his shoulder to get his attention, and told the human, *It is up to us.*

Wait! We need the tribute of fish.

He hurried back to Edon and took his basket of fish from the young hunter. To Eklok, Tostri signed, *If this does not work, be ready to flee.* Before he turned, he felt through his toes the crash of impact.

Whirling, Tostri saw Jagga back away from the tree trunk. He must have thrown all his weight against it. Leaves spiraled from the canopy, and Kurt lay on his stomach on the branch, his head hanging over one side, his feet over the other.

Tostri sprinted past Stanhope. He tilted Edon's basket and spilled its load of smoked fish on the rain-forest floor. The aroma came pouring out, too, an invisible cloud, strong and attractive. Tossing the basket aside, Tostri added the fish from his own container to the pile. He stepped back and signed to Stanhope, *Make the offer! If he charges, run. I will try to distract him.*

Ahead, Jagga leaped toward the branch, his teeth closing on air only inches from Kurt. The angry Suchomimus came back to earth with a crash. Its tail lashed back and forth. Then it sniffed. Suddenly, it whirled, crouching, all its attention drawn by the piles of fish.

Stanhope Ramos stepped forward, holding his arms up, his hands clenched in the deinonychid gesture of truce. "Breathe deep!" he said. "Seek peace! Jagga, we bring you a tribute!"

The towering predator shook its head and roared a

word or two that Tostri could not follow.

Stanhope spread his open hands. "We do not come to take food from you. We do not want your hunting territory. The one in the tree is my son. He is hurt. We wish only to leave you in peace. In token of our respect, we bring you these fine fish, all for you, taken by my friends across the river. Make truce with us! We will leave you to find peace your own way."

The Suchomimus stalked closer, its nostrils flaring. Tostri saw a thin drool drip from the front of its snout. The piles of fish lay invitingly on the forest floor.

A stride away, the theropod paused. It rumbled something else, and Stanhope replied, "Yes, you could eat the fish and attack us, too. But we come in peace. We want nothing from you but your patience in letting us take my son away. You are larger and stronger. We could not fight you if we wanted. Still, where we come from, it is a sign of strength and nobility for the stronger creatures to help the weaker. Have we truce?"

The predator considered for a moment. Its black tongue flicked, licking its lips. Then it said something else. It took one more step and darted that long snout forward. For a terrifying moment, Tostri thought Jagga was snapping at him. Instead, the theropod caught up just one of the smoked fish, flipped it into the air, and, with a stab of its head, caught and swallowed the morsel.

Stanhope looked at Tostri. "We have a truce only

until Jagga finishes the fish," he said. "Hurry!"

The two of them ran to the base of the tree. Stanhope looked up and yelled, "Kurt! Climb down! We have to get away from here now!"

Tostri saw Kurt's staring eyes, wide in a pale face. The boy tried to say something, but the syllables meant nothing to Tostri. He signed, *Climb down quickly! We must hurry!*

To Tostri's bewilderment, Kurt reacted by climbing back onto his branch and clutching at one of the dangling vines. Kurt reeled, his face red. He tried to speak, but Tostri could not read any words from his lips. Stanhope touched Tostri's shoulder and said, "Something's wrong with him."

Tostri looked apprehensively over his shoulder. Eklok, Ezkar, and Edon had not moved. They were still far away, on the other side of Jagga. The Suchomimus stood crouched over the pile of fish, staring at Tostri and Stanhope with hostile brown eyes. Very deliberately, as if to remind them of how short the time was, the predator snapped another fish into the air, then swallowed it.

Desperately, Tostri signed to Kurt: *Hurry! Our truce lasts only as long as the fish last! Hurry! Come now!*

Kurt swayed, breathing hard. He closed his eyes and clung to the vine. Faintly, Tostri caught the scent of dried blood.

Stanhope Ramos leaped and caught at the end of one of the hanging vines. He turned to Tostri. "I'll have to climb up," he said, his expression grim. "If Kurt doesn't try to get higher, I may be able to bring him down. I don't think he knows who we are."

No time! Tostri signed. *No time for this!*

"What choice do we have?" Stanhope asked. He began to climb without waiting for an answer.

CHAPTER 14

Kurt did not notice the newcomers into the clearing until after the Suchomimus had jarred the tree so hard that he lost his grip and fell to the next lower branch, hitting it hard. The wind huffed out of his lungs as the branch caught him across the abdomen. Only by a miracle did he manage to hold on to the dangerous perch, his feet hanging on one side, his head and arms on the other.

Stunned for a moment or two, he could not move. His lungs heaved, trying to bring in air. The sharp teeth of the carnivorous dinosaur clashed together so close that drops of its saliva peppered his hands.

Then he heard a human voice, though the words were in the dialect of the large predators: "Breathe deep! Seek peace!"

Kurt scrambled back onto the branch as a bearded man and one of the deinonychid hunters stepped into the clearing, the hunter pouring baskets of fish onto the forest floor. Something about them was familiar.

He almost knew these two, though something about the dinosaur, perhaps its red neckerchief, was strange, different.

Panting, Kurt clutched one of the hanging vines and stared down while the newcomers spoke to the predator. He could understand a word here and there: *truce, fish, son.* His mind whirled, though, and dizzy with nausea and fever, he could not put the pieces together enough to understand. At least the enormous Suchomimus had turned away from him. It strode toward the Deinonychus with the red neckerchief. For a moment, Kurt thought it was about to attack. Then it seized a fish and ate it, and the man and the smaller dinosaur ran to the base of the tree.

The man called something to him. The words meant nothing. Kurt knew this bearded face, though. The healer—but the healer had brought hunters with him! The dinosaur beckoned to him to climb down, but a fearful glance at the feeding Suchomimus gave Kurt the feeling again of being prey. The theropod could snap him up as easily as it did a salmon. In those gigantic jaws, he would have no chance at all.

Then the bearded man grabbed a vine and began to haul himself up, hand over hand. Was he fleeing the Suchomimus, too? Kurt stared down, and something in the man's expression registered. He understood.

"Father!" Kurt shouted, his voice rusty and harsh. "No!" He held tight to the vine. "I'll come to you."

The climbing man halted, staring up at him. Kurt swung off the branch and began to slide down the vine. The effort was too much. He blacked out almost at once. With a gasp, he felt himself falling, falling thirty feet to the ground—

Oof! He landed on something yielding, something that kept him from breaking his neck—the deinonychids! They had come past the feeding theropod and had gathered beneath him to break his fall. Kurt rolled to his feet. Both he and the dinosaurs had collapsed on impact, and the deinonychids lay sprawled, one of them apparently dazed. He remained on the ground as the others rose, gesturing urgently toward him to flee. On the verge of running, Kurt heard the fallen dinosaur take in a deep, shaky breath. And then—

"T-Tostri!" Kurt shouted. He reached to help pull his friend up.

But Tostri had no time for greetings. *Run!* he signed. *Follow your father! I will come behind!*

"This way," Stanhope said, grabbing Kurt. The big man sprinted across the clearing, carrying his son. Behind him came the deinonychids, retreating, backing away as they held their spears at the ready. They passed the Suchomimus and the rapidly dwindling pile of fish. The big predator roared at them, speeding them on their way.

They emerged from the shadow of the rainforest and onto the bank of the river. With the three strange deinonychids taking the lead, Stanhope and Kurt in the middle, and Tostri bringing up the rear, the party scurried along, following the curve of the stream. Kurt heard a roar behind him.

"He's finished the fish," Stanhope grunted, his face red with effort. "Now our truce with Jagga is over. He'll be on us in no time."

The three hunters splashed out into the stream, and Stanhope plunged in after them. Kurt felt the current tugging at him, and he saw that Tostri was now at his father's side, holding on to his arm, helping the heavily burdened human keep his balance. They had to swim for a short space, but then they all found their footing again. The party stumbled ashore on the far side of the river.

Kurt looked back. The dinosaur his father had called Jagga was on the bank of the river. It bellowed after them and shook its huge head. He felt they had been warned.

What happened next was a blur to Kurt. He did not exactly lose consciousness, but things seemed to happen out of order, and his exhausted mind could not put the pieces together. He had a confused sense of being carried on a litter by two of the dinosaurs, of a glowing fire, of a soft bed of grasses.

Then there were little flashes of pain as his father did something to his hand. Sleep, and then food, a thin soup. More rest.

The next thing Kurt knew, his father was bending over him, holding an earthenware vessel shaped strangely for a human mouth. "Drink this," his father told him. "I think it will help."

Kurt sniffed. The liquid was pungent, thin, and green. Its taste was surprisingly bitter, so bitter that it puckered his mouth, as if he had bitten into cotton. "What—what—" he tried to ask, but everything swam away, and he was asleep again.

And then he drifted for a long time. At last he opened his eyes and stirred. Kurt could see now that he was in a hut of woven saplings. A hanging curtain of leather was the doorway.

With a soft groan, Kurt sat up in bed. He held up his injured hand and saw that it was swathed in a bandage. He flexed it experimentally. It felt stiff, but no longer sent jolts of pain up his arm. Kurt tried to sit up, and in an instant, his father was at his side. The healer's face was thin and pale, the eyes pinched with worry. But it relaxed into familiar lines when Kurt smiled.

Wordlessly, Stanhope hugged him. Kurt felt his father's shoulder shake and understood that the healer was sobbing with relief. "I thought I'd lost you," he whispered. "Kurt, do you recognize me again?"

Kurt lay back and nodded, hardly able to speak himself. "I know you, Father. What happened?"

"You had an accident," Stanhope told him. "Some bad bruises and scrapes, but I think the worst thing was that you got stuck by a poisonous plant."

Memory rushed back then. Kurt sat up on the mat

of grass. "The earthquake," he said. "I fell down the cliff. Is Tostri all right?"

"He's fine," Stanhope said with a grin. "He's become a hunter, your friend Tostri. The deinonychids of Outer Island will have a legend to tell of the silent one!"

"There was a theropod," Kurt said slowly. "I don't think it was civilized."

Stanhope's smile faded. "Jagga," he said. "A Suchomimus, and not a friendly one. I'll tell you all about him later. How do you feel?"

Kurt thought about that for a moment. "Sore," he confessed. "And sort of weak."

"Strong enough to travel?" Stanhope asked, his tone serious.

"I—yes, I suppose so." Kurt looked at his father. "Why? Do we have to leave right away?"

Stanhope nodded. "We've been on Outer Island for five days now. The weather is changing, and Eklok says storms are coming."

"Eklok?" Kurt furrowed his brow. "Who's that?"

"He's the hunter whose camp you're in," Stanhope explained. "A friend. His followers have promised to help us get back to the *Cloudclimber*. We'll have to hurry to beat the storms." Stanhope picked up Kurt's leather specimen bag. "You know, you were lucky you held on to this, son."

"I don't remember what I put in it," Kurt admitted.

Stanhope opened it and showed him a tangle of dried plant shoots, each of them spiked with hooked thorns. "It's a new specimen entirely," Stanhope said. "At least it is to me. And it will be new to the botanists in Dinotopia, too. You will have the honor of naming it, son, since you discovered it. I'm—I'm very proud of you."

"What is it?" Kurt asked.

"Eklok's people know a little about it. They call it the deathtrap plant. It's carnivorous, like a Venus flytrap or a pitcher plant. It seems to be adapted to life as a saprophyte, growing in some of the trees in the rainforest. It gives off a sticky, sweet sap that attracts small insects. When birds come to feed on the insects, the spiny tendrils snag them and inject a venom that paralyzes the victim."

"It seemed to grab my hand," Kurt said, flexing his bandaged right hand.

"Yes, the fronds curl when prey touches them," Stanhope said. "Then, after the spines have paralyzed the bird or the small mammal, the plant feeds on the body. It's a fascinating adaptation."

"It tried to eat me?" Kurt asked.

Stanhope laughed and clapped him on the shoulder. "You were too big a meal for it! But the poison in the spines did affect your memory and your senses. It took me a while to figure that out, but I put it all together after taking the thorns out of your hand and comparing them to the ones in your collecting bag.

You know, I made the medicine that cured you from the plant."

Kurt made a face. "It tasted awful!"

"But it worked. It's funny how the things that can hurt you can often help you as well. It all depends on how you use them."

The curtain over the doorway twitched aside, and Tostri looked in. Kurt had to smile at the sight of him, for in addition to the red scarf, Tostri wore a headdress of woven reeds with plumes of leaves stuck into it like feathers. *Well again?* Tostri signed.

"I think so," Kurt assured him. "I remember now. You gave Jagga the fish, and you helped catch me when I fell."

Tostri's eyes narrowed in amusement. *Ouch! Don't remind me! You are much heavier than you look.* He turned toward Stanhope. *Storms today, Eklok says. Jagga has gone far toward Brightfire Mountain, the hunters report. We must get back to Cloudclimber very soon.*

"Kurt?" his father asked. "Think you can help us beat the storm?"

"I hope so," Kurt told him.

His father patted him on the shoulder. "Good. We still have some unfinished business to talk about, you and I. About the path you will take. But for now"—the healer stood—"for now our path has to take us to what safety we can find."

A moment later, as if to chasten his hope, a rumble of thunder rolled across the earth.

CHAPTER 15

They ran before the coming storm. Kurt wanted to help, but with his injuries, he felt pretty useless. Two of Eklok's hunters wore harnesses that supported a stretcher, and for most of the way, Kurt lay on the stretcher. He kept insisting that he could walk, but Tostri warned, *We have to hurry. You would have a hard time keeping up. Rest for now.*

Before long, they came to the foot of the ridge, and there at last Stanhope helped his son off the stretcher. "Thank you," he said to Eklok.

"Breathe deep. Seek peace," responded Eklok. "Now you hurry to your place. We hurry to ours."

"This way, Kurt," Stanhope said. "Need help?"

"I can make it." Kurt looked up the slope. It was steep, and he would have to creep on all fours, but he was determined to make the climb unassisted.

Up and up, with Tostri before him and his father behind. They broke out into the humid air above the rainforest canopy. Then Kurt could see how dark the day was, the sky a deep, dangerous purple-gray toward

Brightfire Mountain. A streak of lightning split the sky, and an instant later, thunder shook the earth.

"We'll have to get out of here as soon as we reach *Cloudclimber*!" Stanhope yelled above the noise. "We're too exposed up on the ridge, and it's far too dangerous to remain here."

They reached the crest of the ridge and hurried down its spine. Kurt saw that their sky galley waited, intact but sagging a little. The gasbag had lost some helium. Stanhope grabbed the essentials from their camp, taking special care with the willow cuttings. Meanwhile, Tostri hauled out a cylinder of helium and Kurt connected it. The gas hissed into the balloon, which began to crinkle and to strain at its mooring ropes.

"Is one cylinder enough?" Kurt asked as he disconnected the hose.

"It will have to be," Stanhope replied. "Get in!"

He climbed into the gondola, too, and he and Kurt cast off the mooring ropes. The sky galley instantly began to climb, circling away from the ridge as it caught the morning breeze toward the sea. They turned their back on the gathering storm as Tostri and Kurt pedaled with all their strength. Kurt hoped they had reached the blimp in time. Behind them, thunder boomed and crashed. The wind picked up in gusts, and soon they skimmed along the ridge, on course for Culebra.

For an hour, it seemed their luck would hold.

They were flying fast, far faster than they had on the journey inland. The ground dropped away as they left Rugged Ridge behind, and twice Stanhope vented a little helium to keep them from rising too much.

But then the storm hit. It came as a dark sweep of wind-driven rain, a black squall as the sailors called it. The rain and wind tossed *Cloudclimber* the way Jagga had tossed a salmon before snapping it down. The gondola swayed wildly. Kurt gasped as cold rain pelted his back. The downpour hid everything. He could barely make out the blurred ground far beneath as the gondola pitched back and forth.

"Pump!" Stanhope ordered from his place in the bow. Kurt relayed the signal to Tostri, and they redoubled their efforts at pedaling. Kurt felt lightheaded from the effort, and his legs seemed like dead weight. He forced them to move, though, knowing that movement was vital.

Stanhope was trying to keep steerage way. The *Cloudclimber* was caught in a current of air, a fierce wind that threatened to spin it, pummel it, rip it to shreds. As long as they could go just a little faster than the wind, Stanhope had some control. If they slowed, the sky galley would be at the mercy of the storm— and storms had no mercy. Kurt's legs ached with effort, and his breath came in burning gasps. After his illness, he lacked the stamina to pedal at top speed for very long.

They dropped still lower. Finally, Kurt heard his

father shouting: "No good! We're off course. We'll have to land or be swept out to sea!"

Kurt felt a chill that had nothing to do with the rain. The seas around Dinotopia were notoriously treacherous, with deadly crosscurrents and hidden reefs. If the wind carried them out over the ocean, they'd never get home again. Kurt pumped as if his life depended on it—until the pedals jerked to a stop that almost threw him from his seat.

He spun around and saw that Tostri had felt the same impact. Tostri tried to start again, but the pedals were frozen. Tostri signed, *No good. The chain has broken.*

Kurt felt the sky galley slew and pitch as the wind took possession of it. He grabbed for a rope. "Father! The drive chain broke!"

"We'll have to set down here!" Stanhope bellowed. "Kurt! Can you climb down the rope ladder?"

"I think so!" Kurt threw open the chest and uncoiled the ladder. Tostri prepared the counterbalance. "Port or starboard?"

"Starboard!" Stanhope shouted. "Take a mooring line! Make us fast to the strongest tree you can find!" He reached above his head, venting more helium from the bag.

Kurt's legs almost failed him. *I can't do it,* he thought. *I don't have the strength!* But if he couldn't manage the climb—Kurt looped the end of the mooring line around his shoulder. Tostri stood by with the counterweight, but Kurt shook his head. The sky galley was only twenty feet above the tops of the trees. It dropped more as Kurt perched on the edge of the gondola. Rain lashed at him, blinding him.

Then the land dropped away suddenly, and in a momentary lightning flash, Kurt saw a wild landscape below. They had just cleared the edge of a cliff, and now the sky galley dropped even faster. Ahead, not very far, was the white-streaked chaos of the sea.

Kurt felt the sky galley slow, spinning. His father had dropped them behind the shelter of the cliff, momentarily finding shelter from the gale. This was their only chance!

Kurt swung from the gondola, not using the rope ladder but clinging to the mooring rope. He heard his father shout his name. He had no time to think. A sturdy palm tree leaned just ahead, and Kurt hit the ground just at its base. He whipped the mooring line around the trunk, making two hasty but secure half hitches. The rope tightened at once, and from the galley above him, another line spiraled down. Staggering with weakness, Kurt lurched to a second tree and tied the line. Stanhope was venting helium, and the gondola all but crashed to earth. He and Tostri clambered out of the gondola, both weighed down with specimens.

Kurt's vision was blurred. He saw the lightened craft leap back into the air again, up to the level of the palm tree's fronds, before the mooring lines stopped it—

An instant later, the storm boiled over the cliff. *Cloudclimber* thrashed and bucked. The closer mooring line snapped with a sound like an explosion. The unbalanced craft spun and thrashed against a tree. The gondola split, showering the earth with splinters and bags of rations. Another gust tore the sky galley completely free.

Kurt fell to his hands and knees in the rain. With a sinking heart, he saw the craft whirl madly off, rising on the wind, heading out to sea. He followed it with his gaze until the squall hid it.

Then he must have passed out. The next thing he was aware of was being carried by his father. He struggled to say, "I'm all right."

Stanhope set him down at the base of the cliff. "No, you're not. You're still sick and weak. But we'll wait out the storm here. Then we'll head toward the ocean. We should hit the coast road before very long."

The two humans and the dinosaur crouched beneath a rocky overhang that offered little protection from the storm. At times Kurt doubted they would make it. Once, lightning struck the cliff face not far away. The wind grew so fierce that the three of them had to clutch each other and lower their heads against its fury. A brief hailstorm pelted them with stinging white globules of ice.

Then, as suddenly as it had come, the storm swept past, trailing gray skirts of rain. Kurt watched it go. He felt soaked, exhausted, and sore—but his father got to his feet. "Let's go."

They scavenged some of their fallen supplies. Then, with Stanhope supporting his son, they made their slow way toward the seashore, picking their way through wind-damaged trees. Wet brush slapped at them.

But at last, like the storm, their bad luck blew away. They stumbled from the underbrush onto a broad paved roadway. Before them the ocean, restless after the wind and rain, surged in high, roaring surf against a sandy beach. The road curved to their left and right, following the coastline, hugging the edge of the forest. "This way," Stanhope said, moving to the left. "We should be only a few hours from Culebra."

Kurt didn't say that he doubted he could walk for even one hour. Luckily, he did not have to. After only a few minutes, he saw a sturdy log building off to the left of the road. Outside it, a crowd of men and dinosaurs milled about. One of them saw Kurt, Tostri, and Stanhope, and shouted to the others.

For a moment, Kurt was afraid they were just a hallucination, but with a rush of relief, he saw they were real. Two men, a woman, a hadrosaur, and two sturdy Triceratops had found shelter from the storm in the way station. They explained they were fruit harvesters, and they were returning to Culebra with their

130

haul of mangoes, papayas, and other delicacies. The Triceratops carried enormous packs of the fruits, slung over their broad backs. One of them immediately volunteered to carry Kurt as well.

And only when he was riding did Kurt fully realize how tired he was. Part of him wanted to take up that matter of unfinished business his father had mentioned. Most of him, though, cried out for sleep. As the sun came out, warming him, he began to sink into a doze. He hoped that this adventure was over at last.

EPILOGUE

Are you sure you are recovered? Tostri demanded, as he had every day for a week.

Kurt laughed. "I'm sure." The two friends were strolling on a plaza in Waterfall City, surrounded by the bustle and excitement of one of Dinotopia's chief settlements. "Mother even lets me go outside now, so I must be well!"

Tostri nodded. *And have you talked with your father about what you want?*

Kurt looked down. "No," he admitted. "Somehow it's harder now than ever. He saved my life. I owe him everything."

You owe yourself something as well, Tostri replied. *Remember, you kept us from being blown out over the ocean during the storm.*

"Maybe you're right," Kurt admitted. "And maybe soon I'll be able to talk to Father about it. But I'm not ready yet."

Like a good friend, Tostri did not press the point. They arrived at a graceful stone building, one of the research halls of the healers. Inside, they found Stan-hope Ramos standing at a broad window. On a table before him, dozens of earthenware pots held green saplings. "Hello, you two," the bearded man said with a grin. "Kurt, are you sure—"

"Yes!" Kurt laughed again. "Yes, I'm all right. Are these your willow cuttings?"

Stanhope beamed. "Sixty-one out of seventy-two survived. I'll transplant these next season, some to the greenhouses, others to the wild. They should ensure a steady supply of fever tea for years to come." He put a hand on Kurt's shoulder. "Speaking of cuttings, come with me. I've got something else to show you."

He led them into a solarium, a room flooded with sunlight. Saplings grew from large pots scattered all across the floor. Stanhope gestured to one, a young ficus. "Look what else is growing."

Kurt saw that in a crook of one branch a small green patch of tendrils clung to the tree. He shivered. "The paralyzing plant?"

Stanhope took a stylus from his pocket and gently touched the saprophyte. Its tendrils immediately curled, clenching to grasp prey. "It isn't an evil plant, Kurt. Nothing in nature really is, I think. Its venom gives it a way of living. But it could have other uses as well. I think that if it is carefully collected and prop-erly prepared, the venom could be used as a medicine, too. It could be used as an anesthetic, taking away pain. It seems to control infection, too. I don't understand how, but finding out will be one of my tasks." He smiled at his son. "And I wouldn't have had that task to enjoy without you. Even while you were hurt and confused, you held on to your collecting bag."

Kurt nodded. "I just had the feeling that it was important, somehow. I'm glad I got it back safely."

Tostri gestured: *We are glad you got back safely. That is more important!*

More weeks passed. On a sunny afternoon, Tostri and his parents met Kurt and his for a picnic in the countryside. Kurt felt fully recovered, and he and Tostri had races, went wading in a clear, warm stream, and played a blindfold game that Tostri always seemed to win.

At the end of the day, as they were packing to return to Waterfall City, Kurt's mother, Elaina, said with a smile, "I think we should tell them."

Tostri looked at the adults. *Tell us what?*

Etros, Tostri's father, said, "Stanhope has informed us that Kurt would like to train with the Explorers, as you plan to do. We have all been considering that."

Kurt felt his heart beat a little faster. "But I'm apprenticed to my father," he said. "I'm supposed to be a healer."

Stanhope Ramos put his hand on his son's shoulder. "Kurt, my only wish is that you walk the path of life you choose. What you did on Outer Island shows that you enjoy seeking medicines better than using them. Your training brought you through. If you could survive on your own—well, you must have it in you to become an explorer."

Etarah, Tostri's mother, added, "And our son, the silent one, loves to learn about the world around him. We think his way, too, is that of an explorer. We are glad to send him to study with those who go forth to learn. We are more glad that his human friend may go with him."

Tostri turned to Kurt. *It's what we have always wanted!*

Kurt was almost too happy to speak. "Yes." He reached out to straighten the red neckerchief that Tostri wore proudly. "Both of us can learn to be hunters—hunters who do not kill. Breathe deep, Tostri. Seek peace."

And Tostri added one phrase to the traditional words: *Learn new things.*

ABOUT THE AUTHOR

BRAD STRICKLAND has written forty-five novels, many of them for younger readers. His books have appeared on the Bank Street Best Books list, the New York Public Library's Books for the Teen Age list, and *Smithsonian* magazine's list of recommended books. When he is not writing, Brad works as a professor of English at Gainesville College in his home of Gainesville, Georgia. He is married to Barbara Strickland (with whom he sometimes cowrites books), and they have a daughter, Amy, a son, Jonathan, and a daughter-in-law, Rebecca. They also have too many pets, including two dogs, four cats, two ferrets, two fish, and a gerbil.

Like almost everyone else, Brad has always been fascinated by dinosaurs and other ancient animals. As a teenager, he loved to read books by Roy Chapman Andrews, a famous dinosaur hunter. He was thrilled to be able to take this trip to Dinotopia!